THE
IMP
THAT ATE
MY
HOMEWORK

LAURENCE YEP

THE
IMP
THAT ATE
MY
HOMEWORK

Drawings by Benrei Huang

HARPERCOLLINSPUBLISHERS

Library of Congress Cataloging-in-Publication Data
Yep, Laurence.
The imp that ate my homework / by Laurence Yep ; drawings by Benrei Huang.
    p.   cm.
Summary: Jim teams up with his grandfather, who is known as the meanest man in
Chinatown, to defeat a powerful demon.
    ISBN 0-06-027688-6. — ISBN 0-06-027689-4 (lib. bdg.)
    [1. Grandfathers—Fiction.   2. Chinese Americans—Fiction.   3. Demonology—
Fiction.   4. Supernatural—Fiction.   5. San Francisco (Calif.)—Fiction.]   I. Huang,
Benrei, ill.   II. Title.
PZ7.Y44Im   1998   97-11652
[Fic]—dc21   CIP
                                                                                    AC

Typography by Al Cetta
5   6   7   8   9   10
❖
First Edition

To Cory, who's impish herself

—L.Y.

Contents

The Meanest Man in Chinatown

My teacher, Ms. Mason, told my class to write about our grandparents. I put up my hand. "My grandmother is dead," I said.

"Is your grandfather alive, Jim?" she asked me. Reluctantly I nodded my head. "Then you could interview him," she suggested.

I was afraid she would say that. Half of the class lived in Chinatown. They looked at me sympathetically. They knew my grandfather. They knew it would be hard to write about him.

Nobody liked Grandpop much. He spoke his mind and had a sharp tongue too. So he was always getting into a fight with someone. On any given day, he feuded with half of Chinatown.

Sometimes it was his roommates. Sometimes it was the people in Portsmouth Square. Or it was some new waiter at his favorite restaurant. Or it was some tourist who had photographed Grandpop without asking his permission.

Dad said there were ten thousand ways to pick a fight, and Grandpop knew them all. By now people knew to find Dad or Mom, and they would calm Grandpop down.

Last month a tourist's car had almost run over him in the crosswalk as he tried to cross Grant Avenue, the busiest street in Chinatown. Grandpop hammered on the car hood with his cane. Then he started smashing the headlights. When he got tired, he stood in front of the car so it could not drive away. He halted cars for half an hour. The big traffic jam spread into downtown San Francisco.

It had taken both my parents to make him leave. They had had to pay for all the damages. They had also had to explain to a lot of doctors that Grandpop wasn't really violent. He just didn't like fools, and that included careless drivers.

Grandpop and his bad temper had always made me feel uncomfortable, but after that I was really scared of him. And everyone began to call him the meanest man in Chinatown.

I knew I couldn't write about any of that for my essay. My parents would have died of shame.

That night I cooked the rice. Dad brought home half a roast duck from the butcher shop where he worked. Mom got home a little after him. Then she fried the vegetables quickly for dinner.

When we had sat down at the table, I said, "I have to write about Grandpop for school. Is there anything nice to say about him?"

Dad defended Grandpop right away. "He's the most honest person I know. He always speaks the truth. And he gets mad at people who don't."

"Is that why he picks fights with everyone?" I asked.

Dad fished around the plate. "He never fought with your grandmom."

Grandmom had died long before I was born. "I wish I could have met her."

Mom put the drumstick on my plate. Dad never let them cut the drumsticks up even if Grandpop said it was wasteful to give such a large serving of meat to one person. "Everyone liked her. She was such a sweet woman."

The door to our apartment slammed open and then shut. Dad never bothered to lock the door when Grandpop was due for dinner.

"Just in time," Mom said in Chinese, and she got up to get him a bowl of rice.

Grandpop limped over on his cane toward the table. "I've lost my appetite."

Dad sighed as he drew back Grandpop's chair. "Who is it this time?"

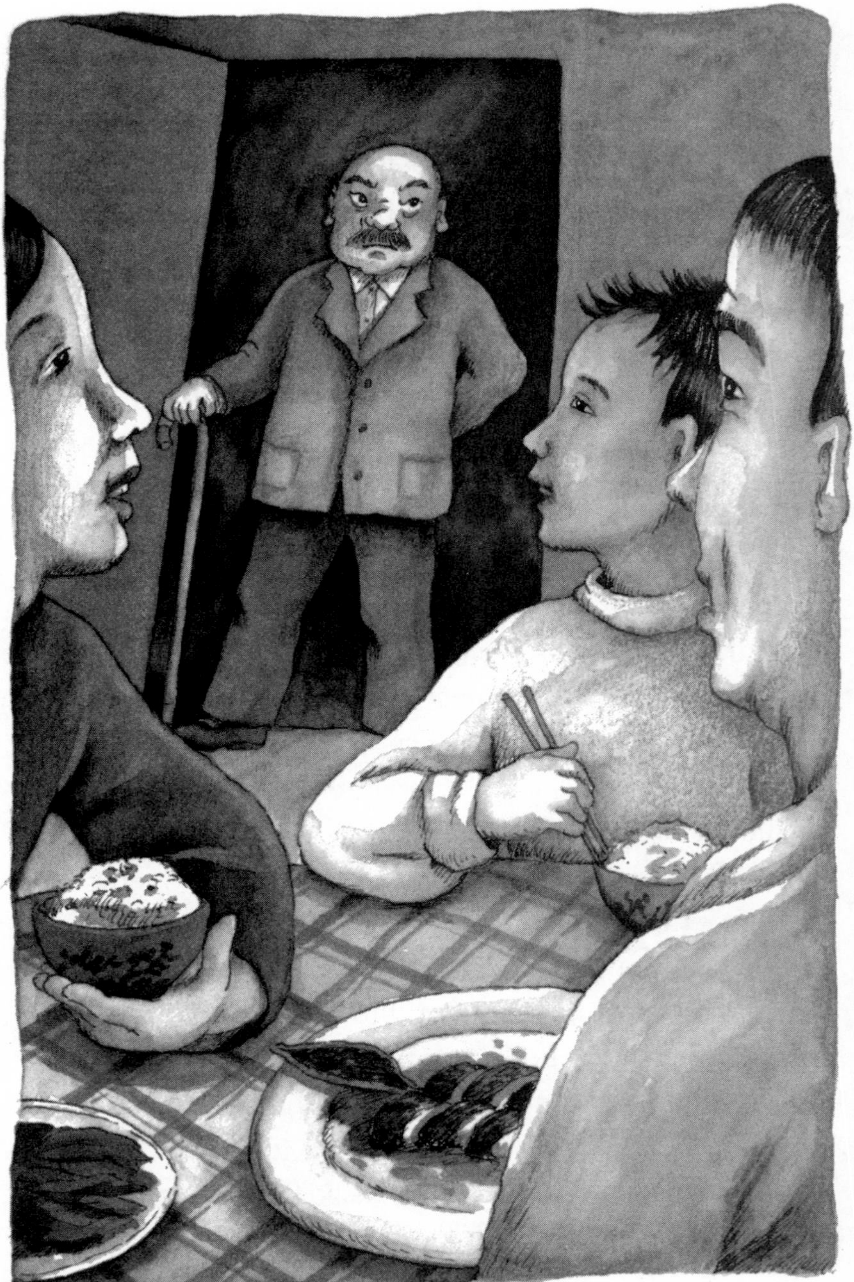

"That idiot Yang," Grandpop grumbled as he sat down.

Mr. Yang was one of Grandpop's roommates. We were trying to get Grandpop an apartment in our projects, but there was a long waiting list. Right now, he shared a tiny room with Mr. Yang and another man. Grandpop was always moving from place to place, though. His outspokenness got him into trouble with one set of roommates after another.

Mom set the bowl of rice in front of him. "Just try to relax now," she soothed him. "A good meal will take your mind off things."

Grandpop stared at the bowl. "Rice should be fluffy, but look at that stuff. It's all mushy and soggy. Why do you keep using a rice cooker?"

"Because it saves time," Dad said patiently.

Grandpop, though, knew the real source of the trouble. He glared at me. "How come you don't wash and cook the rice in a pot? I showed you how to do it the old way. You're Chinese. Why don't you act like it?"

Grandpop was always scolding me. I was pretty tired of it.

Grandpop added, "Native-born, no brains." Unlike Grandpop, I was born here, which made me native-born. He made it sound like it was all my fault.

"If you clean the rice the Chinese way, you'll

wash all the vitamins away," Mom explained, defending me. With her own chopsticks, she picked up the duck's head and deposited it on Grandpop's plate. The head had been cut neatly in half so you could see everything in it. "There, your favorite."

"Do you need to sleep on our couch tonight?" Dad asked.

"No, I'll sleep at home. I didn't say anything too bad this time," Grandpop said.

"Ms. Mason never lets us fight, Grandpop," I said.

Grandpop leaned forward toward me. "What do you see in my face, boy?"

I was so startled, I almost fell out of my chair. I gripped the table while I studied his face. I saw his wide, crooked, flattened nose. Grandpop's forehead was thick and bony, and he had the bushiest eyebrows I had ever seen. He looked ugly, but I didn't say so. I didn't want him to scold me.

"You look like you," I said carefully.

He scowled. I'd lost points with him. I would not get my interview this way. "You're looking at the ugliest face in Chinatown. And you want to know how it got that way?" Grandpop asked. Without waiting for me to answer, he pointed to a scar on his forehead. "See that?"

I nodded. The scar was too big to ignore.

"I got that when a maitre d' at the Wharf threw

a whole bottle of wine at me. Clipped me real good, too," Grandpop added.

He began to point out other scars and marks. It seemed to cheer him up. Grandpop's face was a map of all the places where he had washed dishes. Though I'd heard and seen it all before, I politely nodded my head.

"So what did you fight about with Mr. Yang?" Dad asked.

Grandpop picked up the duck's head with his fingers. He held it by the beak. "He's always bragging about his son, Chauncey. How smart he is. How successful he is. How he owns a huge house out in the Richmond District. So I finally said to him, 'Then why doesn't Chauncey visit you? Why don't you live with your son, the big shot? How come you're still stuck in this dump with me?'"

I looked away as Grandpop sucked the duck's brains from the skull.

Dad shook his head. "Chauncey was stuck-up even when we were in school. Now he's always in the society pages. Mr. Yang wouldn't fit in with Chauncey's fancy American friends. But you didn't need to remind Mr. Yang."

Grandpop placed the skull right side up on the plate. "I know, I know. But I was just telling the truth."

Dad sighed. "Why pick on poor Mr. Yang? It's

like pulling the wings off a fly."

"I didn't mean to make him cry." Grandpop looked guilty. "It's the waiting that gets to me," he mumbled.

"Waiting for what?" I asked. I thought he meant a place in the projects.

Mom shushed me. "Let your father and grandfather talk."

Grandpop, though, turned to me. "You play basketball sometimes, don't you?"

I thought it was a weird question. "You know I do. I've seen you watching me. But you always leave before I can come over to say hello."

Grandpop seemed embarrassed. "I don't have time for silly games."

"You're retired," I pointed out.

Underneath the table, I felt Mom kick my leg. It was a sign to shut up. Grandpop asked me, "Has your team ever been losing an important game, but you couldn't play?"

"You mean when I've fouled out?" I asked.

He nodded. "Well, doesn't the waiting get to you?"

"A little," I admitted.

He patted his chest. "Well, it gets to me too. It eats at me. I know I can help, but I can only stand and do nothing."

"What team do you play for?" I asked curiously.

"The biggest and the best," Grandpop boasted.

I didn't know what Grandpop was talking about, but even so, I didn't think I would ever get so impatient that I'd be the meanest man in Chinatown. I just knew I had to humor Grandpop. I asked him, "When will you ever get to play again?"

Grandpop rested his hands on his cane and stared at me. "When I'm dead."

Grandpop was always shocking people, but that stunned even Dad and me. Mom tried to make Grandpop feel better. "You're going to live a thousand years." It was a traditional blessing.

Grandpop shuddered. "That's what I'm afraid of."

Mom didn't know how to answer that.

Glancing at the clock, Grandpop got up and shuffled over on his cane toward the television in the corner.

Dad frowned. "Can't that wait till we finish eating?"

Grandpop switched the channel to a Chinese station. "I don't want to miss the Chinese news."

The Chinese newscaster's voice boomed through our little apartment.

"Work was halted today on the construction of a new bank in the city of Guangzhou," she announced. "Workers found the remains of an ancient temple."

Men in hard hats stood in the middle of a

fenced-in field. One of them held up a Chinese vase with some kind of blue design on white porcelain. It was as big as his head, and words ran along one side.

Grandpop squinted as he read the writing on the vase. "A *curse on anyone who opens this vase*." He sat back. "I wonder if that's what happened to it."

"In feudal times, people believed such superstitions, but today we are no longer afraid," the announcer was saying.

As we watched, one of the men broke the seals on top of the vase. Purple smoke suddenly rose into the air, startling everyone.

Grandpop's cane rapped the top of our television. "Can't you idiots read? I should have been there to stop them."

"Are you all right?" Mom asked him.

Grandpop looked nervous, even scared. "You wouldn't understand." He stood up. "I'd better be getting home. I'll need my rest for what's coming."

I still didn't know what Grandpop was talking about. I just knew that I had to question him before he left. "Grandpop," I asked, "may I interview you?"

He shook his head. "Not now, boy."

"What about your fight with Mr. Yang?" Dad asked.

"Suddenly that idiot is the least of my problems. I need to leave," Grandpop insisted, and slammed the door behind him.

Dad stared after him. "He's worked so long and so hard. He ought to enjoy retirement."

"Poor man," Mom said, shaking her head sadly. "He's just getting crankier and crankier."

He didn't look cranky to me. Grandpop had been trembling. He didn't look like the meanest man in Chinatown anymore. Instead, he looked like the most frightened man in Chinatown.

After dinner, I wrote only good things about Grandpop in my essay. I knew that's what my parents would want. I wrote about how Grandpop had loved Grandmom. I wrote about how he came to my basketball games. I didn't think Ms. Mason would like it, though. It was kind of boring. If only I could write the truth about Grandpop, I could make it interesting.

I went to sleep wondering what had frightened Grandpop so badly.

The Imp

When I woke up the next morning, I felt something heavy on my chest. I raised my eyelids ever so slightly. Big mistake. Two eyes, huge as bowling balls, stared back at me. It looked like an imp from my Chinese school textbook.

"I must be dreaming. Imps don't live in America," I muttered, and shut my eyes again.

It didn't help. I knew someone was watching me, and the feeling grew worse and worse.

Then I smelled something funny—like the wet, gassy smell from a clogged sink. The imp puffed against my face. Then he was gone. Then he came back again. The imp was not only watching me. He was close enough to breathe on me. Ugh.

"You're not exactly Prince Charming either," the imp grumbled.

I sat up. "Get out of here," I shouted.

12

The imp rolled to the foot of my bed and righted himself. "Oh, my liver! Oh, my spleen!" He took his wrist in his long, splayed fingers and felt for a vein. "You could have given me a heart attack," he complained. "Then you would really be in trouble."

Looking at the alarm clock on my dresser, he took his pulse. I blinked my eyes open and shut. However, he was still there, and he still looked the same: He was six feet tall with four arms and eyes that were large and red. His body and head were apelike, but two horns sprouted from the top of his head. His ears were so long that they brushed his shoulders. His fur was all green.

"Where . . . where did you come from?" I asked.

"I'm a friend of the family," he said. "I just flew in for a visit, and boy, are my arms tired. *Ba-boom.*" He waited a moment and then waved a hand at me in disgust. "I see he's passed on his sense of humor—or lack of it."

"Who are you talking about?" I asked.

"I'm hungry." He picked up a corner of my blanket and sampled it. He spat it out almost immediately. "What else have you got to eat?"

Looking at his sharp teeth, I hoped he didn't like humans. "Please don't eat me. The kitchen is that way," I said, pointing to the hallway.

The imp guffawed. "Don't flatter yourself. I'd just as soon eat yak meat as little boy, and everyone knows how greasy yak meat is." Tapping a wide-tipped finger against his chin, he looked around the room. "The doc says I need more fiber in my diet."

"What's fiber?" I asked.

"Well, you're a big help." The imp leaped from the bed to my desk. He found my backpack. He probed inside with all four paws, pulling out books and papers. Finally he held up a sheet of binder paper. "Hmm, what's this? 'My Grandfather,'" he read.

"Hey, that's my homework," I protested from the bed.

The imp held up the paper and nibbled at the corner. "Hmm, rather bland," he said. He went on taking small bites. "No wit for spice. No insight for seasoning."

In a panic, I crept on my knees across the bed. "Hey, give that back."

The imp jumped easily to the top of the dresser. With a jerk of his head, he tore off half of the paper and swallowed it. "Awfully dry and wordy."

Desperate now, I hopped off the bed. "Why are you eating my homework? Give me that," I said, while I looked for a weapon.

He finished eating the rest of my paper and belched. "Pardon me. Pompous themes always give me gas." The imp bumped his fist against his stomach and belched again.

My whole room smelled of sewer gas. I started to choke for air. "Dad. Mom," I called out. "Help."

The imp lay on his side, and his belly protruded even more. "They already left for work. You're on your own."

"I'll show you." I dashed to my closet and groped for my baseball bat.

From his perch on the dresser, the imp calmly replied, "Yes, do that. I came to see what you're made of."

I found the handle of a bat. I yanked it and stumbled back out of the closet. Too late I remembered I had lent my metal bat to Miguel. The imp pointed at the foam bat and began to rock back and forth with laughter. "Oh, yes, I'm scared now. You're really going to drive me away with that."

"Get out, get out." I began thumping at the dresser furiously.

The imp sighed, resting on his belly. "Are you the best your family can offer? I was expecting more of a challenge."

"Why are you picking on me?" I complained.

"Your family and mine go a long way back in China," the imp sneered. "I wanted to see if America had made you any smarter, but what's that saying?" He rubbed his lip with a finger. "Yes: native-born, no brains. No wonder your grandfather is ashamed of you."

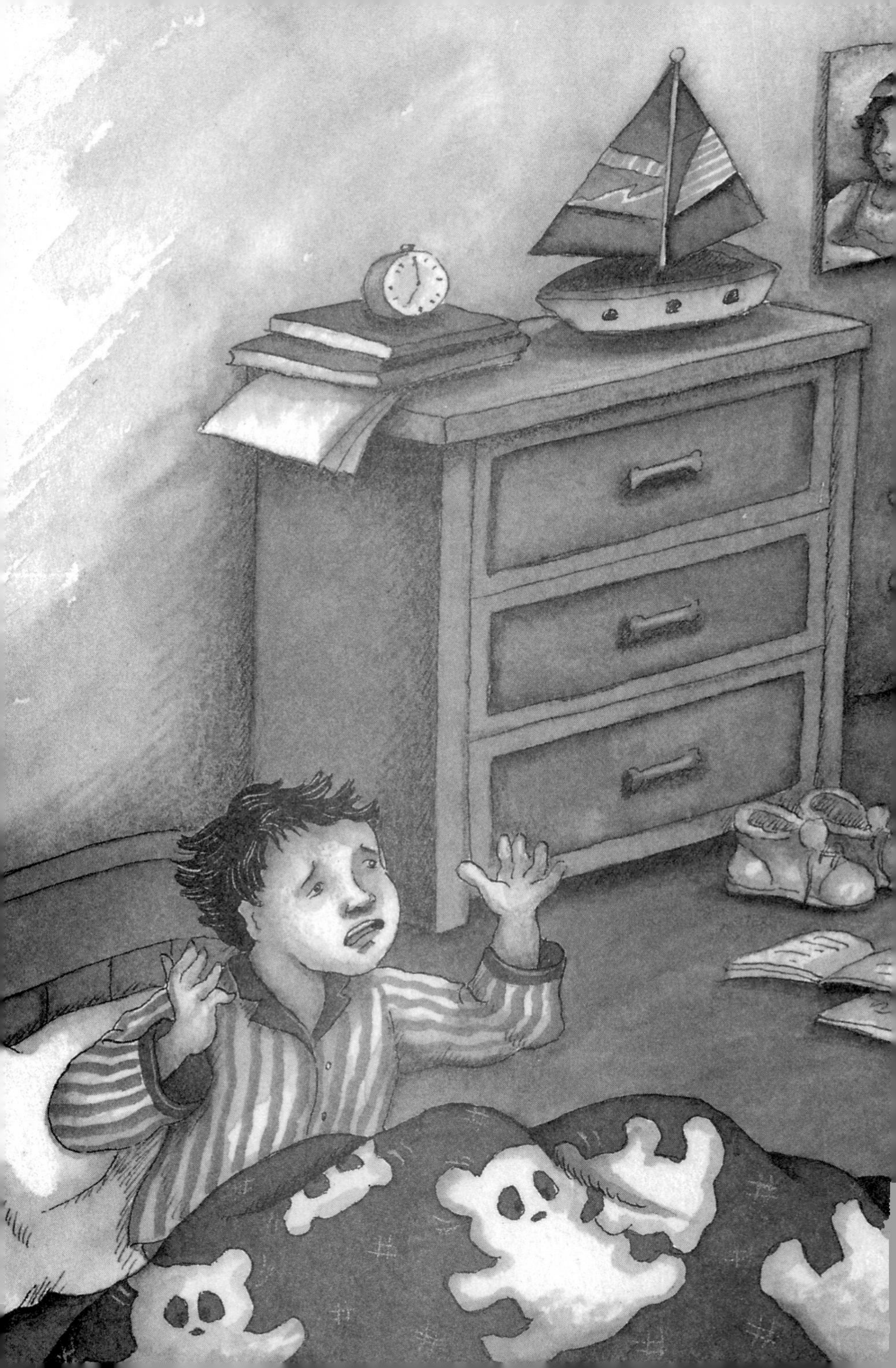

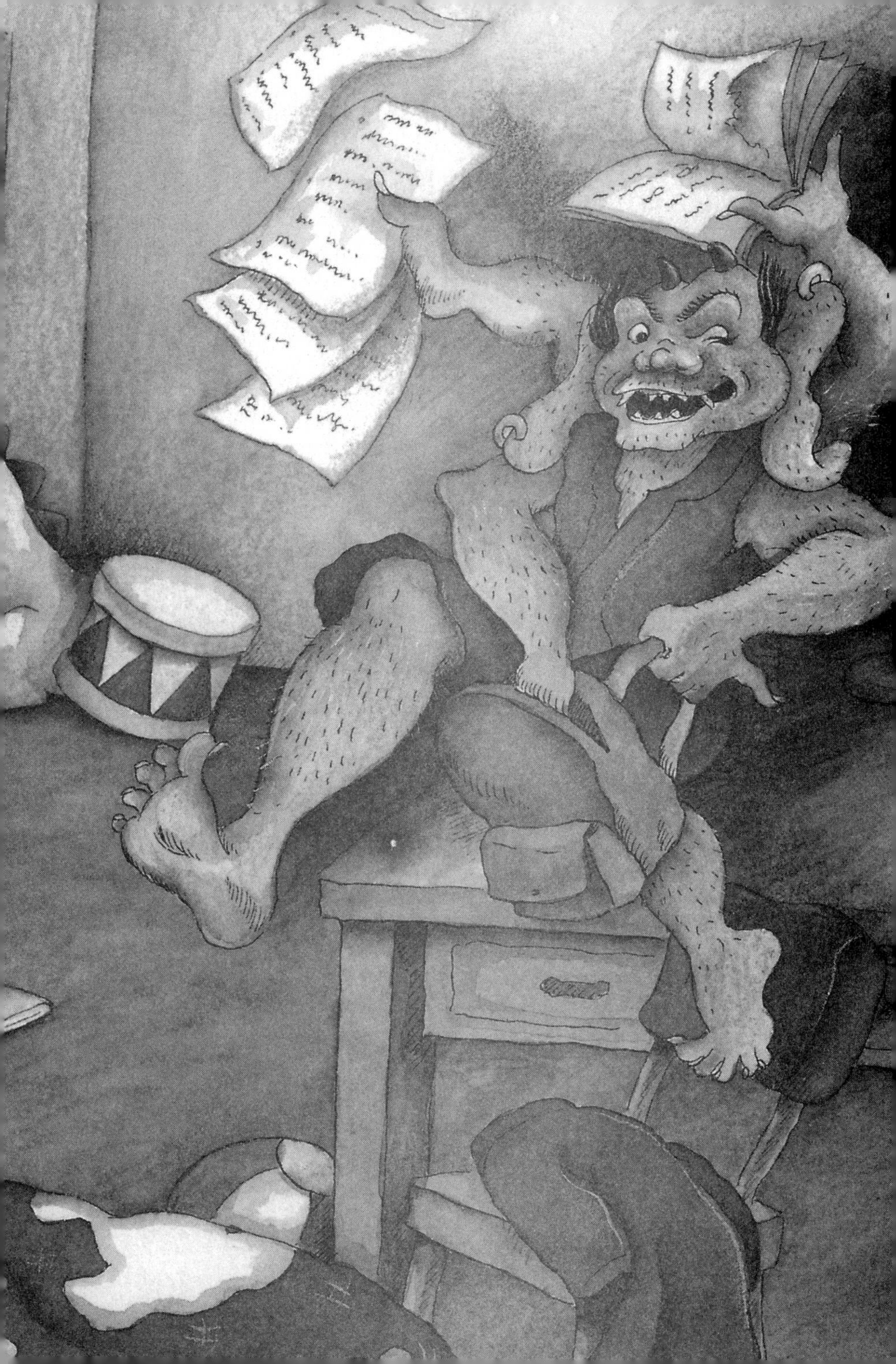

I glanced at the clock. I had to get ready for school. I stuffed my books and papers back into my backpack. I told the imp, "I'm going to call the police. They'll fix you."

When he didn't answer, I looked up at the dresser. He was gone. I looked all around my room and then the apartment. I couldn't find him anywhere. Maybe it was all a bad dream. I checked my backpack just in case. My homework was missing.

The Imp Ate My Homework

I didn't want to be alone in the apartment another minute. I got dressed quickly and then hurried up to school. I figured I had just enough time this morning to write my essay again.

I couldn't figure out why the imp had eaten it. As a prank, it didn't seem very magical or mean. Change me into a goat. Or make flowers sprout from my nose. That's a real prank.

Bullies ruined your homework. Villains with magical powers ought to do something worse.

When I got to school, I sat down on a bench in the school yard. Opening my binder, I found a fresh page. "Dumbbell," a voice whispered in my ear. I looked up and just thought I saw a flash of green fur. When I blinked my eyes, though, I was alone.

Balancing my binder on my lap, I wrote, "My Grandfather."

I couldn't remember what I had written last night. My head felt like it was stuffed with cotton. Was this another of the imp's pranks?

A big yellow school bus pulled in to the curb outside the gates. When the doors opened, my friend Miguel hopped off. He lived to the south in the Mission District but came to Chinatown every day to school.

When he saw me, he headed right over. "Uh-oh. Somebody's late with his homework."

"An imp ate my homework!" I said.

"Sure he did." Miguel winked and plopped down beside me.

"Hey, Sara," he called to another friend. "An imp ate Jim's homework." He pointed exaggeratedly at me.

"Well, he did," I said indignantly.

Sara marched over. "That's pretty lame. Can't you come up with a better excuse?"

"I'm telling the truth. An imp *did* eat my homework." I drummed my pencil against my binder. "If I could just remember what I wrote." Was this part of that imp's sneaky spell?

The imp was smarter than I had thought. People sympathize when flowers grow from your nose. No one cares when you lose your homework.

Miguel rolled onto his back on the bench and kicked his legs in the air. "I wrote about my grandfather. He taught me the bicycle kick."

Sara twisted around so she could read my paper. All she could see was the title, and I knew that wasn't very interesting. "I visited my grandmother in Arizona this summer. She showed me the London Bridge. I wrote about that."

I thought she was making it up.

"No way," Sara said. "They took it apart in England, and then they brought it here—stone by stone. And I will demonstrate how with the next person who makes fun of me." She held her fist beneath my nose, but I knew Sara didn't mean it.

Miguel sided with Sara. "My uncle's told me about the bridge, but I've never seen it."

I thought I heard a faint voice whispering, "Nothing ever happens to you, dummy. You'll never play soccer as well as Miguel. You'll never travel like Sara. You'll always be a joke, just like your mean old grandfather!"

I knew I couldn't write the truth. I tried hard to think of something interesting to write, but nothing came. I looked at my pencil. The point was dull. Maybe if my pencil was sharper, my brain would be too. I got another pencil from my backpack. I tried again, but I couldn't think of a thing to put down.

"You could have all the pencils in the world," the voice whispered. "You still couldn't write."

"Well," I thought to myself, "how about—"

"Nope, nope, too ordinary," said the voice.

"There's always—"

"Not special enough."

I stared at the page a long time. Inside, my stomach twisted and turned like a rubber band. I tried to think of something to write about Grandpop, but the words floated around in my head like old, dead leaves. I snatched at the words, but they always fluttered just beyond my grasp.

"Fool," the voice whispered.

I glanced around. Miguel and Sara had gotten bored watching me and had gone off.

Suddenly the bell rang long, loud, and ugly.

As I walked to the classroom, I felt as if I were wearing concrete boots. Ms. Mason was already at her desk. "Class, take out your essays," she announced. There was a small rumble as we put our books away and pulled out our papers.

Humming, Ms. Mason started to walk down the aisle, collecting the essays. I looked down at my paper. If I told her about the imp, she would laugh just the way Miguel and Sara had.

When Ms. Mason got to me, she took my sheet and stared at it. "How dare you, Jim?"

I was going to tell her about the imp, but I looked around the classroom. Everyone was listening. Everyone would laugh. I was beginning to understand just how sneaky that imp could be.

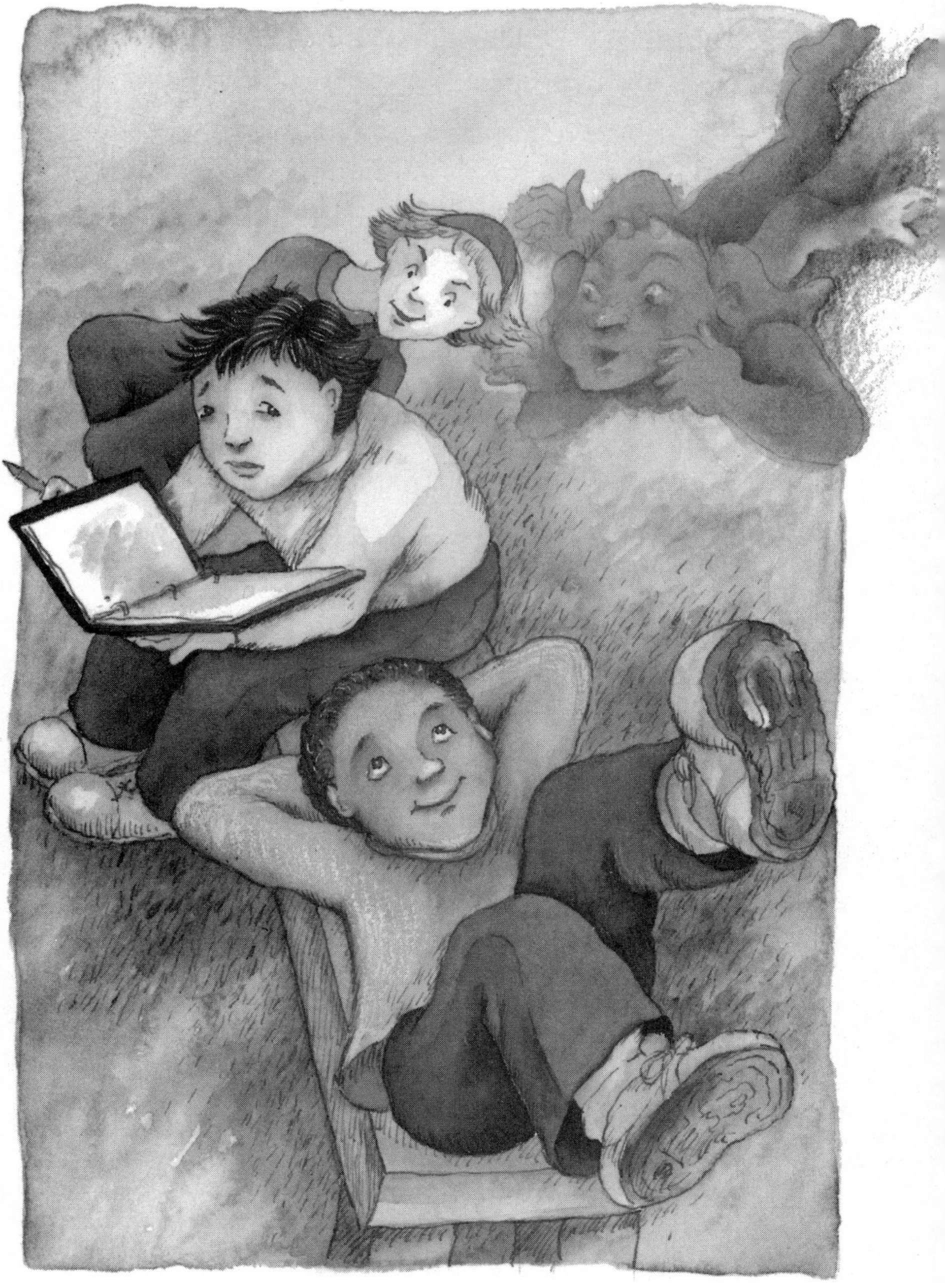

I shrugged. "I'm sorry I couldn't get past the title. There's nothing special to write about my grandfather."

Miguel called out, "You should have asked me for help. I've got lots of ideas."

"No, Miguel," Ms. Mason said. "Jim has enough of his own."

She showed me the essay. Someone had written, "My grandfather is ugly, ugly, ugly, ugly. . . ." The word "ugly" filled up the rest of the page.

"I didn't write that. It must have been the imp," I gasped.

"What imp?" she asked.

So I told her. By the time I finished, the class was laughing.

Suddenly I heard the imp. "Isn't that the stupidest story?" he asked out loud.

Ms. Mason shook her head. "It's obvious you have a good imagination, Jim."

"But I'm not making it up," I insisted.

Ms. Mason frowned. "We have a contract, Jim. You're supposed to do your homework on time."

"Yes, ma'am," I agreed meekly.

"And your parents have a contract with me. They're supposed to make sure you do your homework," she said.

"Yes, ma'am."

Ms. Mason sighed. "I'm going to give you a note.

It will tell your parents that you are in breach of that contract. You must have your parents each read your essay and then sign it."

I slumped in my desk. I was beginning to realize just how cruel the imp could be. "Yes, ma'am."

She thought a moment and then added, "And your grandfather should read and sign it, too."

"But he doesn't read English," I said.

"Then you must read it to him," Ms. Mason said. "And if he doesn't understand English, then you must translate it to him."

Great. Just great.

Chinese School

When school was over, I walked with Miguel to his school bus. "I'll let you have my great-uncle to write about," Miguel offered. As he practiced his soccer drills, his head bounced up and down. "He wears funny costumes and dances the samba at the Carnival."

"I think Ms. Mason would get suspicious," I said.

"A Chinese person could dance the samba," Miguel argued. "Anybody can."

I remembered that morning's encounter with the imp. "What I really need is my metal bat," I said.

"I'll bring it tomorrow," Miguel promised.

"Time to leave, boys," the bus driver said.

Miguel hopped up the bus steps. "Call me tonight, and I'll help you."

The driver worked a handle, and the folding doors shut. Miguel slid into a seat and opened a window with a loud squeak. "If you don't like the samba, I have lots more uncles and aunts and cousins to write about."

I waved as the bus started to pull away. "I'll call anyway," I shouted.

As the bus turned the corner, I started for Chinese school. Classes were at a Catholic school down the hill. When the Catholic school day was done, the Chinese teachers took over.

I hated Chinese school. I didn't see why I had to learn Chinese and all that other stuff. Usually I tried to stay away until the last moment.

However, today all I could think about was the imp. How could I find out about him? How could I stop him?

I went looking for our teacher, Miss Fong.

She liked to wear tight silk Chinese dresses. Up one side was a slit so she could walk easier. She was small, and her hair was always perfectly done. She was also the toughest teacher in school. Almost everyone was scared of her—even the Chinese principal, Mr. Chin. When he visited classrooms, he always corrected the teachers, but never Miss Fong.

I found her in a corner of the school yard. Her pink cashmere sweater was too thin for the cold, so she was shivering. "Miss Fong, do you know about imps?" I asked.

It took a moment for Miss Fong to realize I was talking to her. Usually everyone avoided her. Finally she said, "Yesterday I told the class to read ahead. Didn't you look at today's lesson?"

Too late I realized my mistake. "I . . . um . . . I forgot."

She sighed. "Well, it's about someone who chased away imps."

"Really?" I asked excitedly.

Miss Fong tapped her foot. That was always a sign she was getting ready to lose her temper. "You native-born children are all the same. You never pay attention when I tell you about Chinese history. You only care about ghosts and goblins."

"Let's have a bit more respect," said the imp. I saw him leaning against a wall. "Without me, no one would know about Old Ugly."

"Who said that?" Miss Fong demanded.

"There's the imp," I said, and pointed.

The imp made a face. "Stupid, people can only see me when I want them to." And he vanished.

I dropped my arm. "At least that's where he was."

Miss Fong stared at the wall. Then she turned back to glare at me. She clenched her fingers into a fist. Her knuckles were large and white. Usually this meant she was going to rap a student on the head.

But this time her fist stayed by her side. I couldn't understand why.

"I don't believe in imps, but I do believe in nasty little boys who play pranks," she said.

"I swear I saw it," I protested. However, the more I protested, the more convinced she became that I was lying.

When it was time to go inside, she wagged her finger at me. "Remember," she warned, "behave."

For a change, I didn't have trouble paying attention in Chinese class. I listened as Miss Fong read us the new lesson.

"Chung Kuei was a smart man," the teacher said in Chinese. She folded back the cover of our paperback textbook.

"Chung Kuei was a smart man," the class repeated.

"But he was very ugly," she went on.

"But he was very ugly," we chanted back.

She waved the paper textbook over her head. "Chung Kuei was a very special man," she said to the class, and we recited the sentence after her.

"He passed the government exams with high honors," she read out loud.

"He passed the government exams with high honors," we repeated.

I thought this was going to be another Famous Person story. I got those a lot not only in Chinese school but in American school as well. A famous person usually builds a dam or a bridge or a library. Unfortunately, it was always in a place I didn't know.

As far as I was concerned, famous people were trick questions on teachers' tests.

But I was interested in Chung Kuei because he had chased imps. He had even had an interesting life. Although he had passed his exams with high marks, the examiners had flunked him. They thought he was too ugly. In despair, Chung Kuei had killed himself. Then he had come back as a spirit who chased away ghosts, goblins, and imps.

I wasn't so sure about coming back in another life, though. I put up my hand. "Miss Fong, do you really believe someone can be born again?"

Miss Fong tapped my head with her book. Luckily it was a thin paperback. "Americans don't know everything."

It didn't really hurt, but I rubbed my head anyway. "Yes, ma'am. I'm sorry."

Even if I wasn't sure about the other lives, here was someone to check out.

When we reached the end of the lesson, Miss Fong pointed to me. "Now you read it back."

"Chung Kuei was a smart man," I began, reading in Chinese. For a moment the characters on the page wriggled and danced. When I blinked my eyes, I could see them again. "But his teacher was very ugly."

"What!" Miss Fong demanded as the class laughed.

"But that's what's written on the page," I said. I heard a strange laugh. Looking up, I saw the imp. He was sitting on Miss Fong's desk at the front of the class. "The imp did it." I pointed at him with my book. But when everyone turned around to look, he had disappeared.

As the other students laughed again, Miss Fong narrowed her eyes. "No one likes a clown—especially me."

Shaking, I tried to go on reading. "Chung Kuei was a very special man," I read. "He passed the government exams with high honors."

Miss Fong nodded her head as I read the words.

Suddenly the words on the page began to dance again. I gripped my book tightly, as if I could make the words freeze.

"Go on," Miss Fong said.

Desperately I squinted. "His teacher didn't appreciate him. He was so frustrated that he picked on the poor imps instead."

When I heard the class erupt in laughter again, I crouched, waiting for her knuckles. When I didn't feel them, I glanced up. Miss Fong had tucked her textbook under one arm. She was now rubbing her fist.

"You think you can act up just because your grandfather is the meanest man in Chinatown," she scolded.

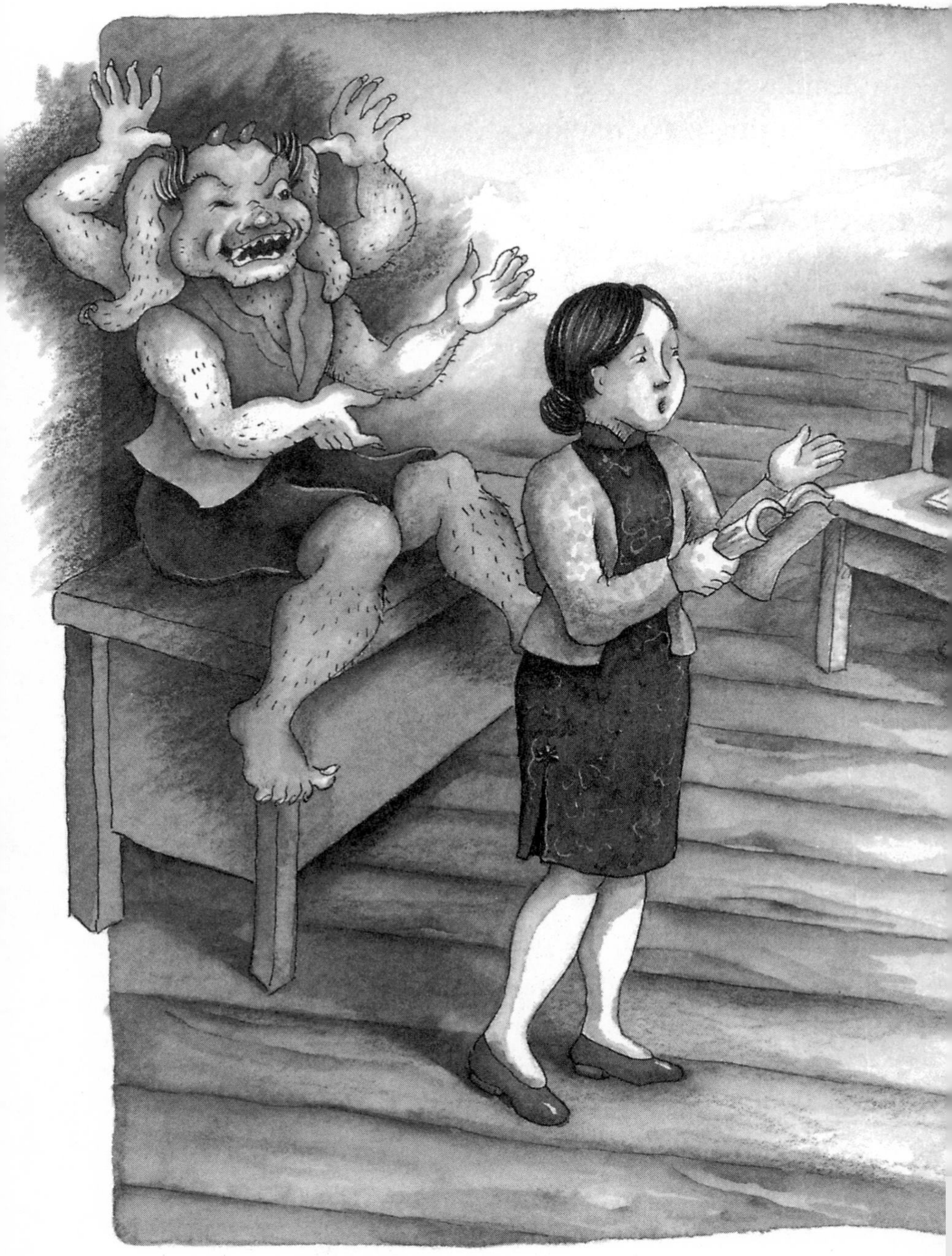

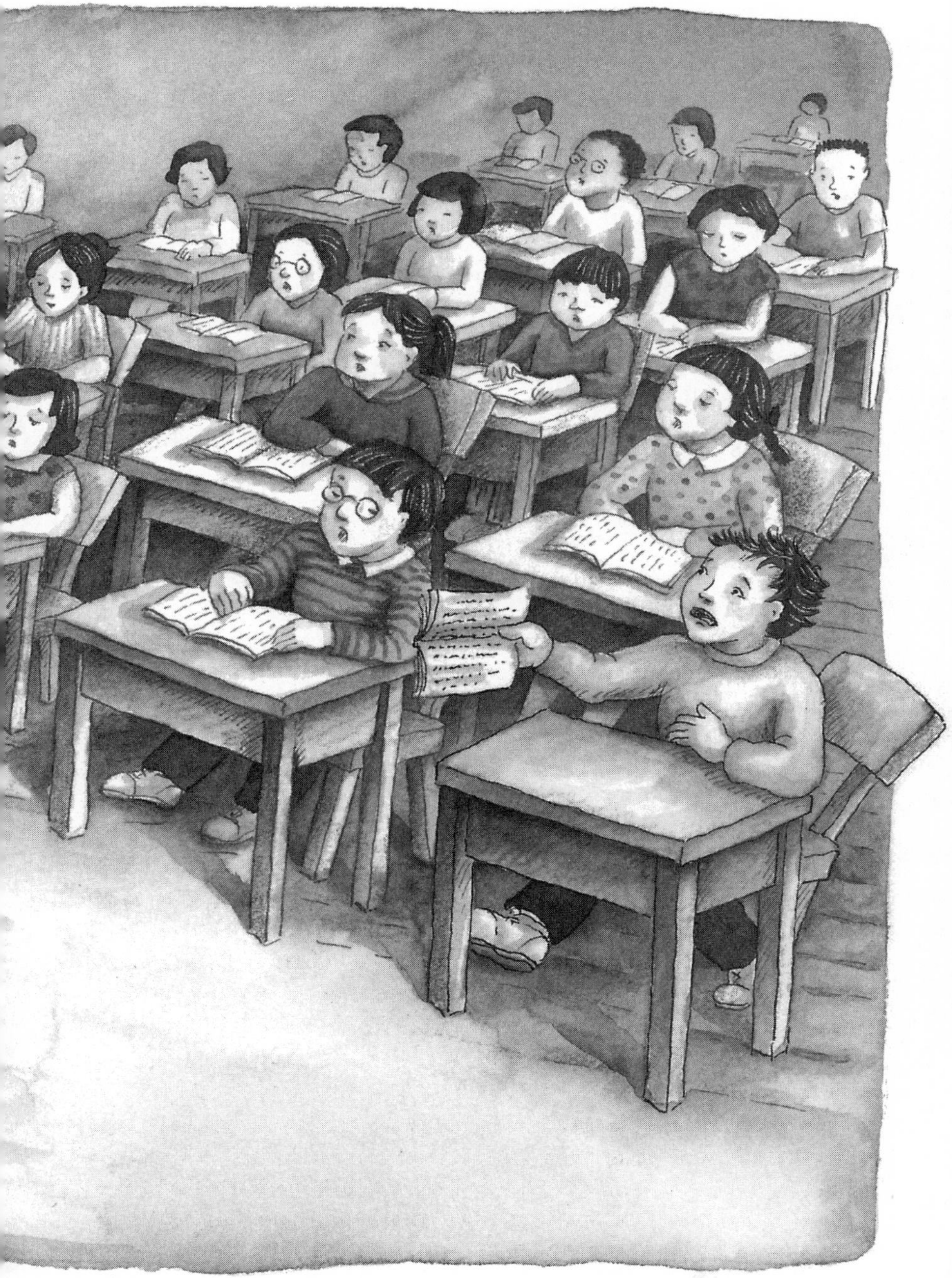

I started to deny it, but then I realized something. Miss Fong was scared of Grandpop.

"Tomorrow I want to meet your parents at school," she told me.

That was a dozen times worse than a note from Ms. Mason. "But they both work."

"I expect to see them both," she insisted. "Let's see how well your grandfather protects you after I finish talking to them."

As she selected another student to read the lesson, I slumped over my desk. I was in even worse trouble now—all because of the imp.

The Sweatshop

When Chinese school let out, I was supposed to go home. Then I was supposed to take rice from the big, red hundred-pound can, put it into the metal bowl of the rice cooker, and wash it. Sometimes there were bits of straw. Sometimes there were even pebbles. When the rice was clean, I would put the lid on and press a switch. The rice would cook automatically and keep warm until my parents got home.

If I had listened to Grandpop, I would have washed the rice over and over until my fingers turned to prunes. Then I would have had to cook the rice in a regular pot and watch it every minute. Otherwise it might burn. I didn't have time for all that old-fashioned Chinese stuff.

But the last thing I wanted to do now was go home. What if the imp was there? I'd be all alone, and all I had for protection was a foam bat.

I thought about telling Grandpop. However, I couldn't figure out which was worse: dealing with Grandpop or the creature. The imp had gotten me in trouble, but so far he had never hurt me. Grandpop, though, could give me a scolding that could hurt as bad as a spanking.

So I went to visit Mom instead. I turned off Stockton and walked down the hill. The sidewalk slanted down sharply. It angled past roofs with curved tiles and neon signs. It wriggled between the huge skyscrapers until it reached the blue water of the bay.

On clear days after a rain, I could see across to Oakland. However, it was hazy today, and Oakland looked fuzzy around the edges.

Stockton had been broad and sunny, but the hilly street was narrow. Even so, the sun managed to squeeze in between the buildings. When I turned into the alley, though, everything was in shadow.

Brick buildings rose on either side. There were storefronts on the ground floors just like the stores on the other streets. However, some big picture windows were covered with used cardboard. Others were boarded up like forts.

There were apartments on the second floors and above. Fire escapes zigzagged up the dirty brick fronts.

On television, I saw where other kids lived. Chinatown seemed so cramped and ugly. Sometimes

I felt embarrassed. Miguel had wanted to come over to my house, but I always found some excuse to get out of it. When I grew up, I was going to live in a nice big house somewhere else.

I stopped in front of the sweatshop where my mother worked. Mismatched strips of material had been hung inside the window. Fluffy lambs hopped through green meadows toward rockets on launching pads. Sharks swam lazily toward stacks of hay drying in meadows. Huge roses tumbled in an avalanche toward houses.

I rang the doorbell. Even through the thick wood I could feel the vibrations of the sewing machines. It sounded like a hive of bees humming.

Miss Gee opened the door. Miss Gee was the boss. She wore her hair in black waves on either side of her head. She used so much hair spray that her curls bounced like steel springs. On her nose she wore a pair of black-rimmed glasses. Miss Gee always wore a raincoat—even indoors. She had one to match her every mood. They had all been made in the sweatshop. Today she was wearing pink.

Some days she recognized me. Other days she couldn't tell me from the other children who were trying to see their mothers.

This afternoon, though, she was in a happy mood to match her coat. "Come on in." She waved me inside with her magazine. She always read the same kind of magazine about houses. This one was called *Gracious Country Living*.

Inside were five long tables. On each table were four sewing machines. They were buzzing and humming, so the women had to talk in loud voices. In the background, someone had turned on the Chinese radio station. A man was speaking, but I couldn't make out the words in all the noise.

Today the women were sewing blouses together. The nylon pieces came in precut triangles and rectangles. From the pieces, each woman would assemble a blouse. The women would be paid for each

blouse they made. This way they got much less than if they worked by the hour.

Mom was all the way in the back. The air was always still and stuffy back there. Even so, she stitched the pieces together quickly. Her foot worked the pedal of the machine while her fingers guided the cloth. At the moment they were working on a print with bright red roses.

The completed blouses hung by the hundreds on clothes racks. More material covered the tables. Roses seemed to fill the entire shop. It looked like a flood of roses, but there was only the smell of dust in the air.

Mom only glanced at me and went right on with her sewing. She was wearing an apron with many pockets. "How are you, boy?"

I leaned against the table and whispered in her

ear. "My Chinese-school teacher wants to see you and Dad tomorrow."

Mom looked at the other women around her, but they hadn't heard. "What did you do, boy?" she whispered back.

"The teacher thinks I did it, but it was an imp. He placed a spell on my textbook," I said.

Mom went back to stitching. She kept her eyes fastened on the machine. "What are you talking about? We put a whole ocean between us and the imps. Those superstitions belong in the old country."

I didn't try to argue. Instead, I dug out the note. "There's more. I need you to sign this."

When I held it out, I saw Mrs. Mar stretch over to peek.

Mom quickly picked up the note. Though she couldn't read English, she recognized Ms. Mason's signature. "More imps?"

I nodded.

She handed it back. "We'll talk about this at home." She didn't want the other women knowing about my trouble.

"I'm sorry."

Mom finished the blouse and put it on a hanger. As she buttoned it up, she said, "Go tell your father now."

An angry father was almost as dangerous as an imp. "Can't I stay here with you?" I asked her.

Mom smiled. "Don't worry. When I see him, I'll remind your father that he was young once, too."

"Thank you," I said uncertainly, "but I'd still rather wait with you." I tried to hug Mom, but I bumped into her machine.

Suddenly I saw a flash of green fur. "There's the imp," I cried, pointing.

But Mom was shouting, "Fire!" Smoke was coming from her machine.

Fire is a serious thing in a sweatshop. The rags and bits of cloth are like dry tinder. Little flames can easily grow into big ones.

"What did you do, you naughty boy?" Miss Gee asked. She came over with a fire extinguisher. "I saw you hit the sewing machine."

"He didn't do anything. Leave him alone," Mom said.

Miss Gee put out the fire. She grabbed me by the collar and gave me a shake. "Your mother will pay for the damages," she said. Then she dragged me to the door and threw me outside into the alley.

The Butcher Shop

What did the imp have against Grandpop? I didn't even know why he was mad at me. But I needed help.

I did what Mom told me and went to see Dad. Besides, I was afraid to go home now. From the alley I cautiously continued down the hill toward Grant Avenue. It was the heart of Chinatown. Chinese waddled along with shopping bags filled with groceries. Groups of shivering tourists dressed in T-shirts and shorts quickly took pictures of one another. Even when it was sunny, it was often cool in Chinatown. The stores that did the best business in Chinatown stocked sweatshirts.

I wound my way through the crowds on the sidewalks. The souvenir stores were jammed with painted metal fish and T-shirts. On shelves behind the fish were statues of kung-fu fighters. Mixed in with them were holy saints, but I wasn't interested in them.

Learning about the saints was even more useless than cooking rice Grandpop's way. It was like Mom had said: We had left all that stuff behind us. She and Dad never talked about it.

Grandpop had tried to tell me about it, but he just made me feel bored. I was a normal American kid. I kept yawning until he finally gave up. He said that if his children didn't care about Chinese culture, his grandson clearly cared even less.

I passed one store that had a fancier sign than most. It stuck out over the street and had green neon sides that curved like Chinese roof tiles. Grandpop had told me it had once been a theater for Chinese opera.

He had seen actual stage shows there with Grandmom. Although there was singing, the performances weren't like American operas. The Chinese actors wore makeup that made their faces look like masks. They also had to fight and do fancy acrobatics. Grandpop said it was more exciting than any action movie, but I didn't believe it.

We had gone inside once, and Grandpop had shown me where the stage and seats had been. I could see their outlines on the floor and walls. Now there were only counters with T-shirts and souvenirs.

Then I walked by a weird bank that looked like a temple in one of my Chinese textbooks. Some tourists were posing for a photo by the two big stone lion dogs in front of the bank.

I figured a bank should look like a bank. This one was ridiculous. Actually, I didn't like any of the Chinese-looking buildings in Chinatown. They made my home look like it was decorated for a year-long Halloween party. Sometimes I felt like my face was just a slant-eyed Halloween mask.

My father worked in a butcher shop next to the bank. It had green tiles and plate-glass windows. In the front windows roast ducks, complete with heads and beaks, dangled head down from their webbed feet. To the left of the ducks was a huge section of succulent pork, the skin roasted a crisp, salty brown. In metal pans over steaming water sat various other dishes—string beans with black bean sauce, sweet and sour pork, and squab cooked in soy sauce.

Ah Wong, the boss, stood in his usual spot in the corner. On his head was a square paper cap, and he wore a yellow apron that wrapped around him like a robe. On his chest was sewn the name "Sam" in red thread. It had nothing to do with his name. He had bought the used aprons cheap. They came from an Italian butcher shop up in North Beach.

As far as I knew, Ah Wong never did anything. His nephews took care of the customers. Since it was beneath him to touch money, his son-in-law took care of the cash register. Ah Wong just liked to stand in his shop with his arms folded, stiff as a statue.

One of his nephews was cutting up a roast duck into pieces. The cleaver made thumping noises as he chopped. Grease splattered the glass splash shield.

I managed to wedge my way in between two customers. "May I see my father?" I asked.

Ah Wong bent his head ever so slightly toward the rear of the store. Since I had his permission, I slipped into the back. I knew what my father was doing when I heard the rhythmic hissing.

The metal door on the huge freezer was shut, and yet I felt cool breezes puffing at my face. The sawdust gave off whiffs of cold meat as I stepped through it.

My father sat in an old chair. Between his tall, black rubber boots he clutched an old bicycle pump. With one hand he raised and lowered the pump handle while the other held the needle steady into the body of a duck.

Before ducks were roasted, the skin was separated from the flesh. That way the skin would be nice and crispy when it was cooked. The fastest way to part the skin from the meat was to pump air between them. When the ducks were inflated, they looked like pale footballs with tiny wings and legs.

Puffed-up ducks hung from hooks behind him. Dad shoved down. *Hiss* went the handle through the pump, and the duck swelled rounder and larger.

Dad wore the same square paper cap as the others, but his apron had the name "Harvey" on it. (Dad's name was Fred.) "Why aren't you home, boy?" When he spoke, his breath puffed out in the cold air.

I told him about the imp and American school and then Chinese school. To my surprise, Dad didn't lose his temper.

"Imps, huh?" Dad went on inflating the duck. "I think you'd better talk to your grandfather," he said.

"Grandpop?" I asked. I had already decided not to ask him for help.

"Sure," Dad said. "He knows about that stuff."

"But he doesn't care about me," I said to him. "Grandpop's always scolding me."

"That's his way of showing he cares about you." Dad winked. "There's more to your grandfather than meets the eye."

Suddenly I heard Ah Wong shouting, "Who let that cat in?" There was a crash, and men began to shout.

The next moment a green cat bounded into the room. It jumped from the floor to my shoulder, where it settled down happily. "Hi, pal." The imp was back, but he had changed into a cat. The imp whispered in my ear, "Remember me?"

Ah Wong stormed through the doorway with a broom. His face was as red as one of his

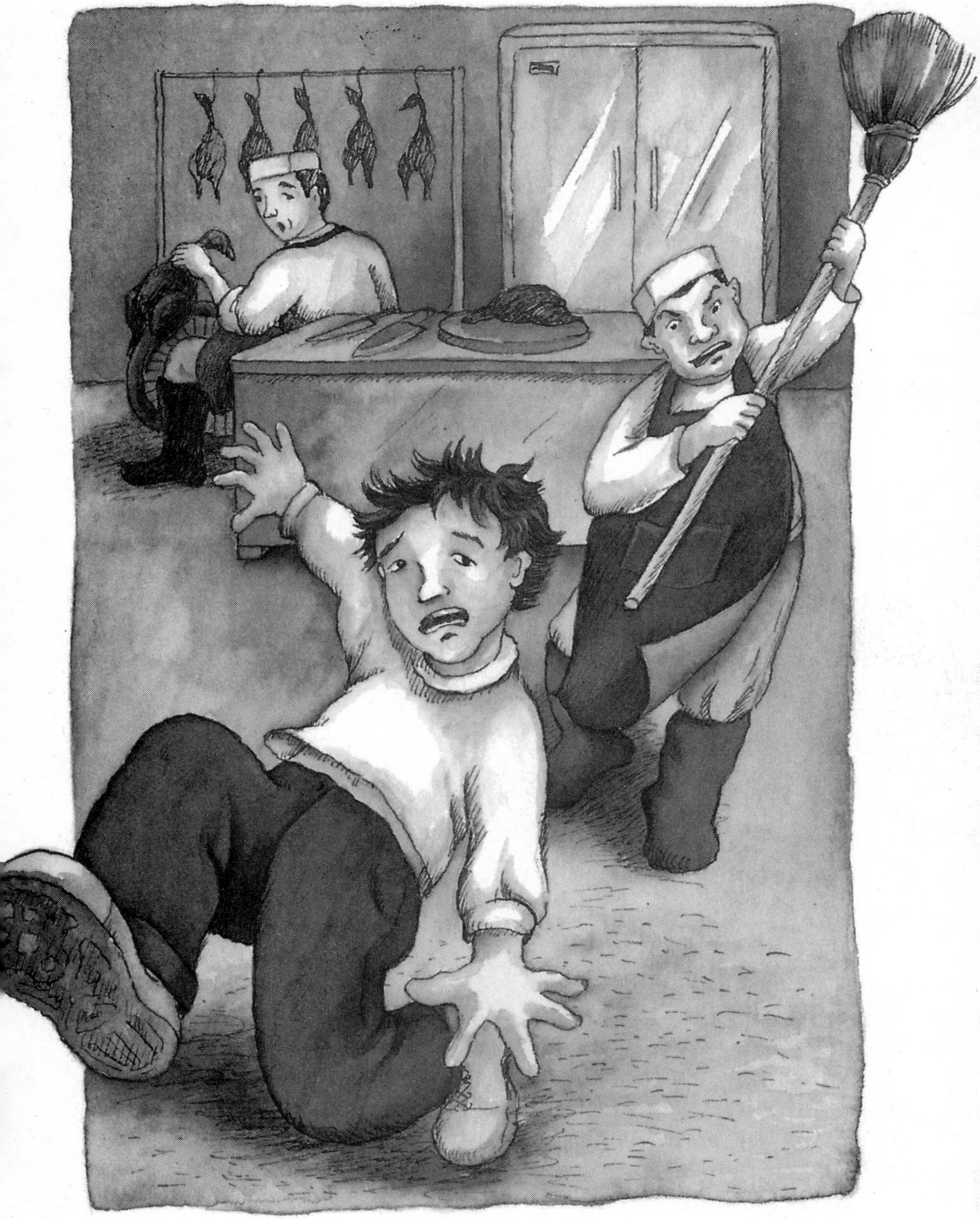

steaks. "So it's your cat!" he said, pointing his broom from the imp to me.

"No, he's not mine," I protested.

The nasty imp licked my cheek.

"Ah, ha!" Ah Wong said, raising his broom. As he stood there panting, the mist swirled around his head.

"It's an imp." I tried to grab the cat, but it slipped out of my hands and jumped to the floor.

"I'll take the costs out of your pay," Ah Wong swore at my father.

I took a deep breath and started to tell Ah Wong all about the imp, but my dad stepped in between us.

"Go find your grandfather," he sighed. Dad gave me a gentle shove toward the door. "I'll deal with Ah Wong."

On the sidewalk, I heard the imp cackle, "Your grandfather's next. Tell him I'm coming."

I looked around for the imp, but I didn't see him. I guess he could be invisible outside, too, just like in Ms. Mason's class. "What are you going to do to him?" I asked.

"I've had lots of centuries to plan everything. He's going to suffer." Suddenly a paw appeared in the air. The claws looked like knives. They slashed through the air with a swoosh. "And so are you."

The next moment the paw disappeared. But the imp's voice echoed against the high sides of the buildings.

Portsmouth Square

Scared, I ran over to Grandpop's place. I hammered on the door with my fist, but nobody answered.

So I cut through the mall. Chinatown couldn't even get that right. Instead of regular stores, the ground floor and the basement had little stands selling more tourist junk. Upstairs they had a fancy restaurant instead of a Happi Burger.

The only booth that wasn't too embarrassing was the pearl counter. You could pick your own pearl there. You wouldn't think anything so ugly could hold anything so pretty inside. But I myself had twice seen tourists pop the plain shells open and lift out glistening pearls.

When I stepped through the door, I was on Brenham Place looking at Portsmouth Square. It was the only other spot Grandpop could be at this time of day.

I stood for a moment looking around. I expected to see Grandpop scolding the others about losing their Chineseness. Most of the elderly people here had been born in China, but even they were too American for Grandpop. I thought they were boring, so I tried to avoid them.

I saw an old woman doing her exercises, and an old man tuning his fiddle. The rest of the old men had gathered around the stone tables near one side of the Square. On the tables were the paper grids for Chinese chess. Disks moved around the red lines. On each disk was painted a word: Elephant. Chariot. Cannon. General. Soldier.

The players sat on the benches while their friends stood around watching. Sometimes the spectators even argued with one another about strategy.

Some of the men wore sweater-coats or jackets. The real old-timers wore Western-style suits. Grandpop owned only one. Every night Grandpop would iron his suit himself so it would be ready to wear the next day. In their dark clothes and stooped over the boards, the men looked like larger versions of the pigeons around their feet.

There was a crowd everywhere except around Grandpop. He was playing chess with Mr. Lee. By now Grandpop would have chased any bystanders away.

Grandpop's grumpy ways didn't bother a

cheerful man like Mr. Lee.

Mr. Lee saw me first. "Your grandson's here."

"What're you doing playing chess?" I asked Grandpop.

A breeze started to blow. Grandpop put his hand on the paper board to hold it in place. "I have to do something while I'm waiting," he said, without looking up.

"Hello, boy," Mr. Lee said in English.

"Hello, Mr. Lee," I said politely.

Grandpop was too busy concentrating to look at me. Mr. Lee threw up his hands. "What kind of grandfather are you?" he teased in Chinese.

Grandpop glanced up at Mr. Lee, and I shivered. Sometimes Grandpop seemed to look right through a person. "I'm no worse than some grandfathers and I'm a good deal better than many." Then he gazed back down at the board.

Mr. Lee, though, wouldn't give up. "A man as homely as you ought to be glad of any love he can get."

Grandpop moved a piece and then sat back in satisfaction. "My grandson doesn't judge me by my looks. I come by this face honestly," he said. "When I work, I work. When I play, I play. Checkmate in three moves."

Scratching his head, Mr. Lee studied the board. "You are a chess wizard."

Grandpop turned to me then, sure that he had beaten Mr. Lee. "Now what is it, boy?"

So I told him about the imp's pranks from this morning until just now. "He said he was coming for you next."

I was surprised Grandpop didn't make fun of me. Instead, he leaned forward, squinting hard. I squirmed at first, because I thought he was looking at me. Then I realized he was staring behind me. "Did he now?" he asked thoughtfully.

"How do we make the imp leave us alone?" I asked him.

Grandpop rested his chin on top of his cane. "Well, you would need a necklace of carved peach stones or maybe a sword made out of Chinese coins," he said.

"How did you learn so much about imps?" I asked.

"Do you think I've washed dishes all my lives?" Grandpop demanded indignantly. I didn't understand how anyone could have another life, but Miss Fong believed the same thing.

"Maybe I'm Chung Kuei in disguise," Grandpop said.

"You're ugly enough to be Chung Kuei," Mr. Lee told Grandpop.

"We just studied him in school," I said excitedly. "He chased imps and ghosts and goblins away." For once I knew what Grandpop was talking about.

"Poor Chung Kuei. He was so ugly that everyone avoided him," Grandpop grunted. "They couldn't see what was really inside."

I remembered today's Chinese school lesson. "Was it because he was so smart?"

"He was smart because he had the gift." He pointed his cane at the air. "He saw things the way they really were. That's how he could protect people from demons and imps."

"How did he do that?" I asked.

"To see the truth, you must look at something

from different angles." He held up his fingers like a window frame and looked at me through them. Then he moved them to the side in illustration.

I took a big step sideways and examined Grandpop from a different angle. "You still look just the same," I teased.

"Native-born, no brains," Grandpop sniffed. "You native-born think you know everything, but it's only the imps fooling you."

He sounded so sincere, he convinced me for a moment. I remembered Dad's advice. Maybe there was more to Grandpop than I had thought. "If you really are Chung Kuei, why did you wash dishes in Chinatown?" I asked.

Grandpop sheepishly rubbed the back of his neck. "When I chase an imp, I forget about everything else. Maybe I got carried away once. Perhaps I even wrecked a palace up in Heaven. So as punishment I got sent down here."

"When you play, you play. When you chase, you chase," Mr. Lee said.

I looked back and forth between Grandpop and Mr. Lee. "Are you joking?"

Mr. Lee started to move a disk forward and then slid it back. "I just know that life is very interesting around your grandfather."

I wasn't sure about anything anymore. I folded my arms. "You're so calm now. But you were so scared last night, Grandpop."

"I was," he admitted, "but then I realized the imp was bound to bring me what I wanted."

"What's that?" I asked.

"An end to waiting," Grandpop said calmly.

"He said he was going to get you," I said.

"Did he now?" Grandpop smiled.

Suddenly I heard the imp again. "Cheat. How could you do this to me?"

The Feud

Grandpop did a double take. "So it really was you in that vase," he said. "Didn't you learn your lesson last time?"

Grandpop's hand brushed the air as if he were chasing away a fly. He stared at something past my shoulder. "Well, do your worst." He almost sounded relieved.

"That would be doing you a favor," the imp snapped back.

Turning, I saw the imp dressed in fancy silk robes.

Raising his hem, the imp danced about. "I've been waiting a long time to get out. And when I do, look at what I find. You're an old broken-down wreck."

I glanced back at the table. Mr. Lee was still studying the chessboard and muttering to himself.

Everyone else in the Square was going on with their games.

"How can they be so calm? Don't they see the imp?" I asked Grandpop.

Grandpop didn't take his eyes off the imp. "They don't see the imp because they're as lazy as you are. The imps tell them what to see, and the imps tell them what not to see. I call the condition Slow-Eye."

"Slow-Wits is more like it," the imp jeered.

Grandpop stamped his cane. "Your quarrel is with me. Why pick on my grandson?"

The imp halted and dropped his hem. "That was just to make you boiling mad, old man. Your grandson was the appetizer before the feast. I've been planning for years to grind your bones into dust. But you let yourself grow old. So what if I can beat up a rag bag like you are now? Where's the glory in that?" The imp plucked at his lip thoughtfully. "I'm changing my plans."

Grandpop squeezed the handle of his cane. "You know I can't use magic in this lifetime. Do what you like with me."

The imp snapped his fingers. "No, the real revenge is leaving you alone while I make your family miserable. Without your magic, you're helpless to stop me."

I shivered though I wasn't cold. "What have we done to you?"

The imp jabbed a finger at Grandpop. "Ask him. He chased and tortured imps for centuries. Now it's my clan's turn to get even."

Grandpop gave the imp his meanest look. "I'm warning you one last time to leave the boy alone. I don't need magic to beat you," he growled, and raised his cane.

"Without magic, you're just full of hot air," the imp jeered.

Grandpop swung his cane, and the imp nearly lost his head.

"You couldn't hit a palace," sneered the imp. Even so, he scrambled backward out of reach of Grandpop's cane.

"Watch me." Grandpop rose.

"You'll be sorry," the imp shouted defiantly as he ran through the park and into the mall.

Grandpop would have followed, but he was puffing like an old train. So I blocked his path. "Let's get away, Grandpop."

Grandpop leaned on his cane. "I don't run from that sort of creature."

"Then let's get some of that magic you told me about," I said.

Grandpop shook his head. "If the imp escapes

now, he will keep coming back and making your life miserable."

I stayed where I was. "Do you think I'm a coward?" I asked.

"It doesn't matter what I think you are. Or what anyone believes," Grandpop snapped. "In my first life, I cared too much about what people thought, and I wound up dead," he said. "After that, I stopped worrying. I just did what I had to do."

I remembered last night. "Does this have to do with the game you were talking about?" I asked.

Grandpop nodded. "But the stakes are the highest, boy. That's why I can't just sit back and watch from the sidelines."

I thought of how I would feel if I had to sit on the sidelines of a game like Grandpop's. Maybe I'd get impatient too. Maybe other people would even call me mean. "But where's your team?"

"Sometimes all you have is yourself," he said quietly.

Now Grandpop didn't seem as scary to me. "Are you really Chung Kuei?"

"The imp seems to think so," Grandpop said. "And he'll plague you and your parents if I let him."

"So you really care about us?" I asked.

Grandpop stiffened. "Where did you get the idea that I don't care about you? Is that what the imp told you? Well, it's a lie!"

"I thought we annoyed you," I said.

Grandpop seemed puzzled. "No. You and your parents are very important to me. You've all made the time pass by much more easily for me. You ought to know that."

I shook my head.

Grandpop rubbed his neck. He looked embarrassed. "I guess I've just been busy feeling sorry for myself and waiting to die."

I stood near, ready to support him. "You don't have to."

Grandpop sighed. "This human thing is harder than it looks. If your grandmom were alive, she would have helped me. And now . . . well, now it's too late."

"It's not too late," I said. "Let's go find my parents."

Grandpop grimly shuffled toward the mall. "I've got things to do first."

Chinatown people said Grandpop was not only the meanest man around, but also one of the most stubborn. "You can't go after the imp, Grandpop. He's got all that magic, and . . . and you're only a dishwasher."

Grandpop tapped his cane against the cement. "I told you, boy. To see the truth, you need to look at something from different angles. But it's obvious that you're not ready. So go home. When I'm finished, that imp won't bother anyone again."

I'd had my fill of the imp for that day. However, despite his bold words, Grandpop could only limp forward slowly. He was a bent old man. He didn't look like a supernatural warrior.

I didn't see how Grandpop could beat the imp. Suddenly I had a horrible thought. What if Grandpop was trying to save the rest of us?

I wanted to run home. I wanted to hide, and yet I couldn't let Grandpop face the imp all by himself. It wasn't bravery. I just knew I couldn't desert Grandpop. I wanted to be on his team.

"Wait, Grandpop," I said, and ran after him. "I'll come with you."

Table for Two

Inside the mall, a clerk at a counter grumbled at the imp, "Hey, you can't ride your skateboard in here." Then he shook his head. "What a weird-looking kid."

"Why did he say that?" I asked Grandpop. "The imp's not riding a skateboard."

When Grandpop turned around, he seemed surprised to see me. "People see what they expect to see," he said, and waved his hand at me. "Now go home. You'll just get hurt."

"You're not tackling that thing alone," I said, catching up to him.

I thought Grandpop was going to scold me. Instead, he scratched his cheek while he studied me. "You're as stubborn as your grandmom," he grumbled. "I'm trying to keep you safe."

Grandpop couldn't scare me away though. Together we moved deeper into the mall. Ahead of us, the imp wove his way through the crowds using the staircase. A couple of German tourists barely jumped out of his way. "Kids," one of them complained.

"*Sprechen sie Deutsch?*" the imp laughed. We chased him up the stairs and narrowly missed a group of tourists eating ice cream. Even so, a cone hit Grandpop in the face. "Sorry," I called back to them.

"Sorry?" Grandpop asked indignantly. "I'm the one who got the ice cream cone in the face." He glared back at the tourists. "If you can't walk and eat at the same time, ice cream is too dangerous for you." He pointed at his coat pocket. "Get the tissues, boy."

I wiped some of it away, but I couldn't resist sampling it. "Hmm, chocolate."

"I prefer tutti-frutti myself," Grandpop said as we stepped onto the next floor.

We wandered among the counters. "Now where is that imp?" Grandpop asked, scratching his head.

Rice suddenly showered down on us. From the restaurant balcony above us, the imp hooted. "Hey, Ugly. Up here."

When we looked up, we saw him waving an empty rice sack. "You're too stupid to know when to stay retired," the imp jeered.

The tourists were looking around, puzzled. "What made it rain rice?"

Rice fell from Grandpop's head and shoulders as he walked into the elevators.

As the elevator rose, we tried to wipe the rice from our clothes. The grains rattled against the floor. Grandpop wriggled. "Darn that imp. I think I got some rice under my shirt."

"Take off your tie and unbutton your collar," I said.

"And have everyone think I'm a bum?" Grandpop protested. Instead, he leaned over so I could help pick the grains away.

When the door opened again, we ran into the restaurant. Suddenly, I saw the clawed foot. "Look out."

Too late! Grandpop tripped over the imp's foot, falling right into a restaurant fountain. Spluttering, Grandpop sat up.

"Look at the little piggy," the imp said. He pretended he was taking a picture. There was a click and a flash.

As the imp skipped away, I ran to Grandpop. "Are you all right?" I asked, holding out a hand.

Grandpop clung to my arm. "That imp will pay for every insult and every indignity."

As I helped him stand, water fell down the folds of Grandpop's clothing. "Come here and fight," he shouted at the imp.

"Nyah, nyah," the imp said, making faces.

"I'll fix you," Grandpop yelled. I hauled him from the fountain.

"Where's your army?" the imp laughed.

Grandpop's wet shoes squeaked as we chased the imp around the restaurant.

Suddenly, the imp waved his paws at a huge tank of crabs and muttered mysterious words. Then he pointed at me. "This boy will be very tasty boiled."

The crabs began to swell. They grew and grew until they were as large as collie dogs. "Or maybe he'd taste better cooked in black bean sauce," the imp said.

The crabs rocked the tank until it tipped over. They swept out with the water and started toward me, clicking their claws.

"Look at those monsters!" Though the customers and waiters didn't seem to see the imp, they could see the crabs.

The imp took a bow but didn't say anything.

Grandpop put his cane on the floor and calmly yanked the tablecloth from the nearest table.

My mouth hung open. The dishes were still on the table. "Where did you learn that?"

"It can get pretty boring for a dishwasher when the restaurant's closed," Grandpop explained. He dropped the tablecloth over the nearest crab and began shoving it with his cane. "Help me, boy."

I ran to the crab and helped turn it around.

Blindly, it charged right into its mates. They immediately began to shove and pinch one another.

"Crabs," Grandpop explained, "have too many grudges. They never make good team players."

Watching the crabs battle one another, I had to agree. Around us, frightened customers jumped to their feet. Chairs clattered to the floor. Tables got overturned. Teapots flew into the air.

The imp tore out his hair and shouted orders to the crabs. "Quit fighting with yourselves! Pinch the boy! Chop up that grandfather."

We skirted the warring crabs. "I don't need magic to take care of you," Grandpop taunted the imp.

With a squawk, the imp flew out of the restaurant, leaving us with the mess and the blame.

We struggled toward the elevator as the red-coated waiters hurled cups at us. A red-faced statue of the god of war suddenly rose up in the little shrine at the back of the restaurant. He kicked over the electric candles and the bowl of tea and threw an orange at us. "Who's going to pay for this? Who's going to pay?" he shrieked.

Grandpop reached into my pants pocket and flung half a dozen coins at the statue. "Here," he said.

Quickly we rode the elevator back down and staggered outside onto the sidewalk.

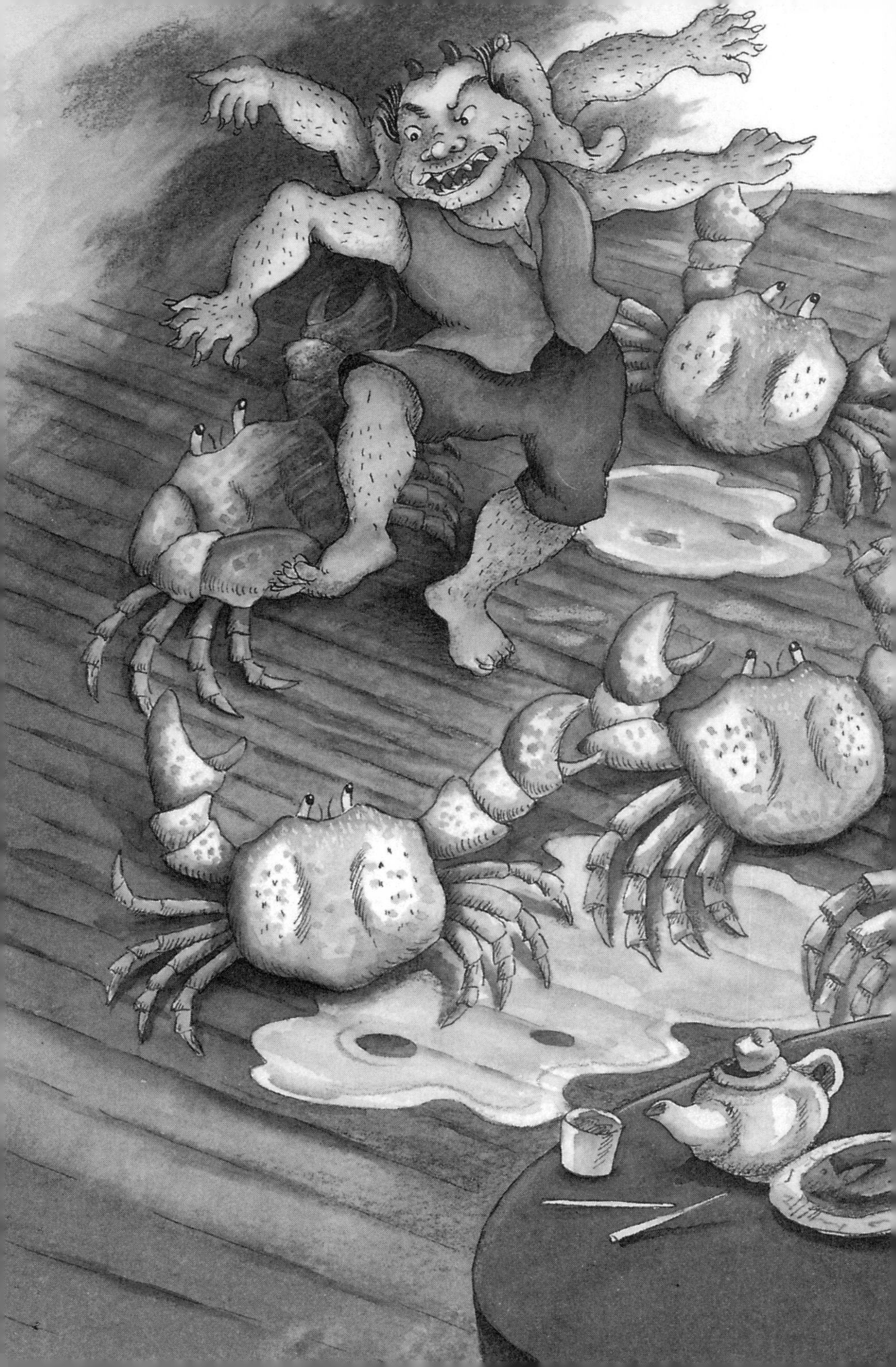

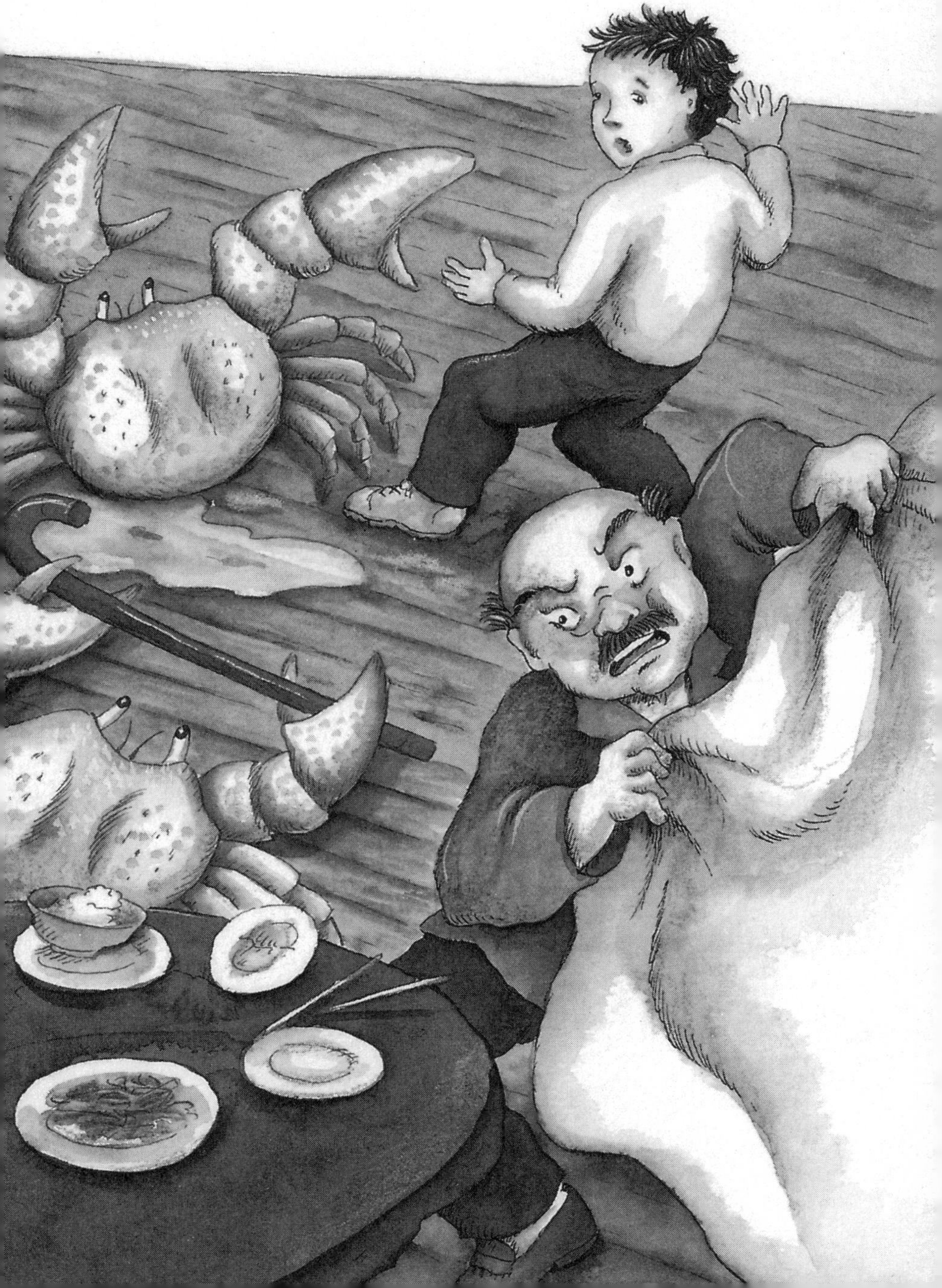

Stage Fright

e caught up with the imp in front of the big store that had once been a theater.

The imp spun around and around on a postcard rack and shouted insults at us. "What kept you, Ugly?" the imp sneered. "You're getting too old and slow for the chase." He began flinging pictures of Alcatraz and the Golden Gate Bridge at us.

Grandpop and I ducked as we moved forward. Postcards spun past overhead.

The imp hopped down and raced inside the store. I tensed as we plowed straight after him. I expected Grandpop's cane to break display counters and send T-shirts flying through the air.

Instead, he pulled me across worn wooden planks with his cane. Lights so bright they blinded me for a moment shone in front of us. Suddenly I heard a huge cheer. Grandpop bowed. He was now wearing a warrior's robes and a grand feathered hat. His face was made up like a Chinese opera star's. Red for loyalty and virtue covered his cheeks. Black stripes covered his eyebrows. They stood for truth and simplicity.

Stunned, I touched my face and felt paint. It was greasy.

"We're onstage, boy. Where's your manners? Bow," Grandpop whispered through his makeup.

I barely had enough sense to do what I was told. "Did you work this magic?" I stammered to him.

"I didn't have to." Grandpop smirked. "Theaters have their own magic. There's still lots of enchantment left here."

I saw the imp standing in the middle of the stage. "After all these years, we can finally finish our feud," he sang. "Are you ready?" He seemed surprised to hear himself sing and felt his throat.

Grandpop's cane changed to a sword. When he twirled it over his head, the blade shone in the theater lights. "You thought you were so clever to take the battle into the theater, but it's just what I planned," Grandpop sang back to the imp.

The imp whirled about on one foot. The next moment he stood in a general's robes. He wore a mask of green makeup.

"Hey, hey demon chaser. Big bully!" the imp trilled. "I'm tired of your ruining all my fun. Stage or street, I know I'll beat you anywhere."

Someone booed from the audience. Someone else shouted, "Where did you learn to sing? At a hog butcher's?"

Grandpop boomed, "The fight will be better than the music. Here we'll battle to the bitter end with no one to interfere."

"To the end." For once, the imp agreed with Grandpop.

The audience began to throw half-eaten snacks at the imp. He winced when a dried plum hit him.

Cheers went up at that shot.

The imp wiped at his face. He snarled at the audience and then at Grandpop. He raised a paw. From one of the wings came an ominous clacking sound. An army of back scratchers scuttled forward onto the stage on their fingers. The plastic stems rattled together like scorpion tails. So that was the noise we had heard. Worse, each stem ended in a wicked-looking hook.

The imp raised another paw. Instantly, flocks of painted fans flapped over our heads, flashing pictures of Great Walls and palaces and gardens before our eyes. Their bottoms ended in spikes.

"You're as ugly as your grandson is dumb!" the imp caroled.

"Quick. Stand back to back, boy," Grandpop whispered.

I heard drums thump rhythmically. A horn tooted angrily, and cymbals crashed.

I didn't take the imp's army very seriously at first. Then I got whacked by a back scratcher's plastic stem. It hurt me badly enough to leave a bruise. Grandpop broke it with a savage blow. "Mind the scratchers' hooks, boy. They're probably poisoned."

Suddenly a band of fans dove at us. "Duck," Grandpop shouted. We both squatted in time as the fans darted past our heads. "Careful of the fans too. They're going for the eyes."

I couldn't believe what was happening. I had a thousand questions for Grandpop, but he was too busy battling the imp's army.

I was surprised at how nimble Grandpop was. The stage seemed to energize him. As he battled fans and back scratchers, he even danced and sang.

I wasn't very good, though. It was all I could do to keep the back scratchers from scuttling around behind Grandpop and stabbing him. I told myself that no one had come to see me perform. All eyes were on Grandpop.

I tried to help. I timed it so that I could grab a scratcher's stem and then fling it into the audience. I didn't know what would happen to them next. Maybe they would turn back into souvenirs. At least I didn't hear any screams. All I could hear was the audience happily snacking as they watched the spectacle.

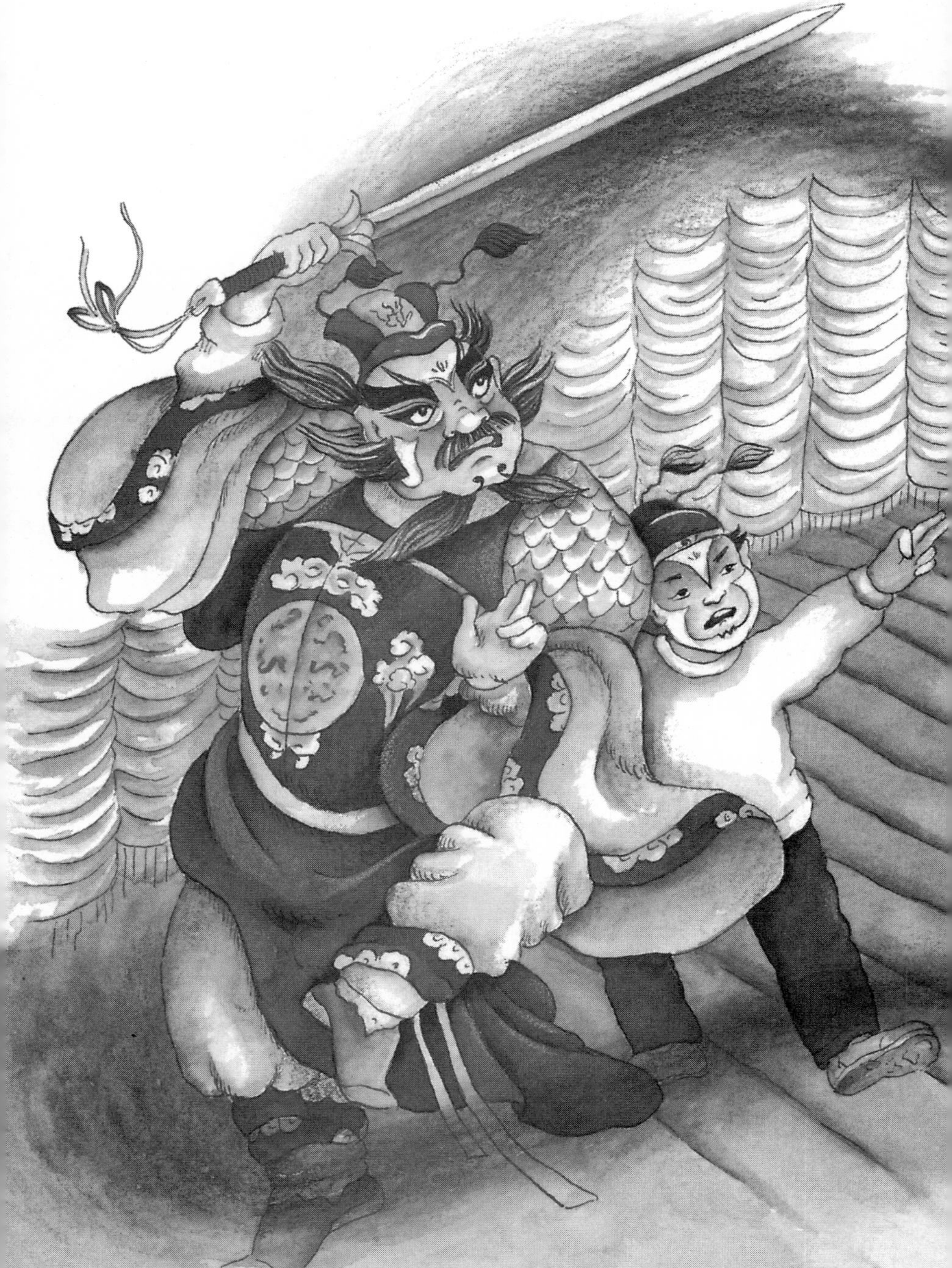

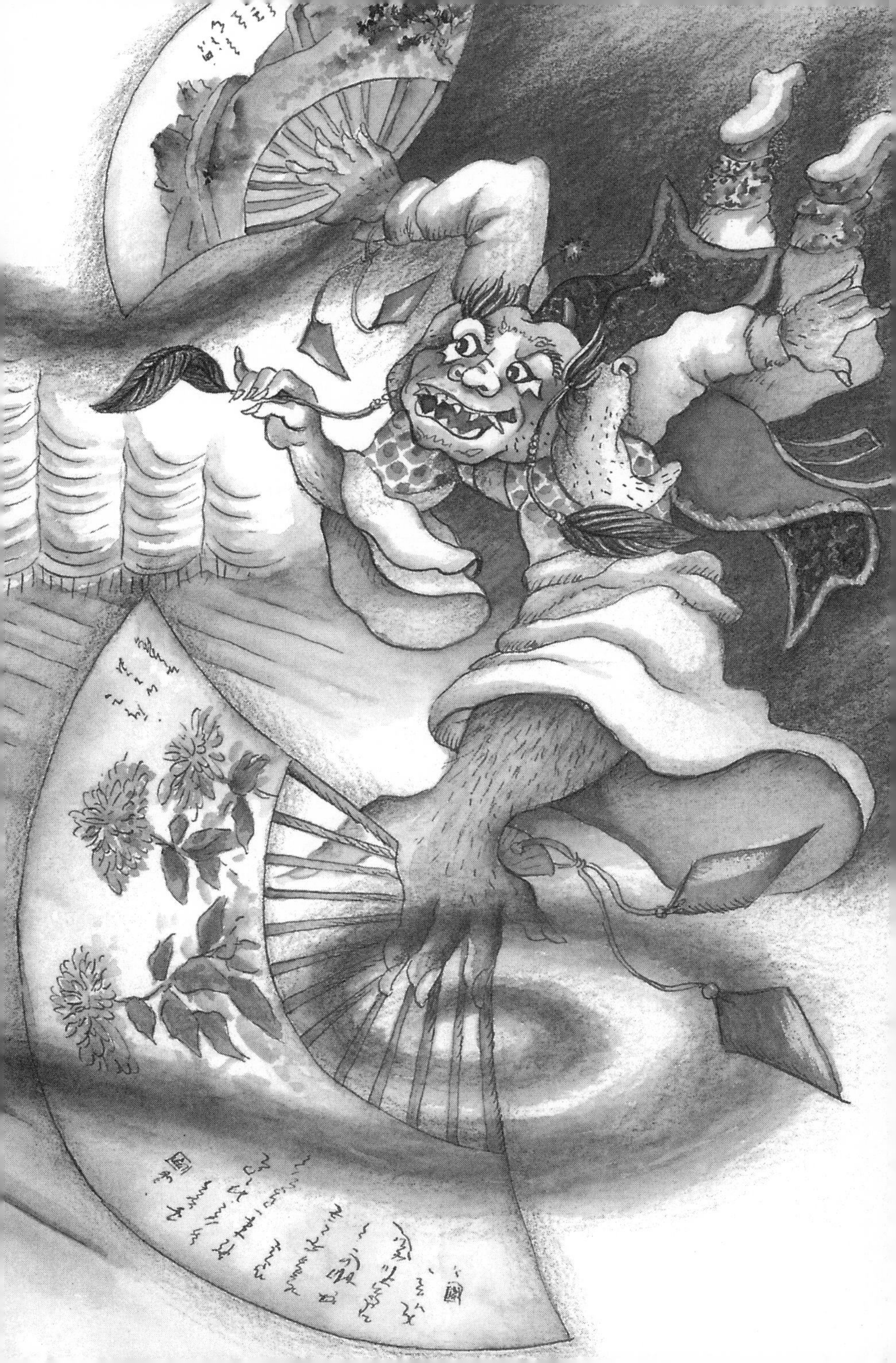

Cymbals crashed and horns tooted triumphantly, and Grandpop scattered the last of the imp's warriors. Raising his sword, Grandpop danced relentlessly after the imp.

He thrust his sword at the imp. Costume and makeup vanished. Frightened, the imp flew offstage.

"Come on, boy," Grandpop shouted. "We've got the imp on the run now."

The Net

When we stumbled outside, it was late afternoon. The sun was starting to set behind
the hills. The buildings cast long shadows across the
streets. The shadows of the fire escapes covered the
street in grids.

Across the street the imp crouched by the bank
between the pair of huge stone lion dogs. For the
first time, he looked a little scared. "You old meany.
You haven't changed any," he whined.

Grandpop tried to hide his limp as he marched
toward the imp. On the street, he had turned back
into an old man. "Do you give up?" Grandpop chal-
lenged him.

"To an old has-been?" The imp suddenly raised
all of his paws defiantly.

The shadows seemed to quiver. I stared at the
shadow of a fire escape. I saw it wriggle like a bunch

of snakes. The shadows were moving.

The imp gathered them in his paws, and the shadows heaved up and down. Then one shadow lashed out, wrapping itself about my ankle. It felt cold and sticky, like tar. I tried to pull it off, but the shadow clung to me like glue.

Frightened, I turned to Grandpop, but other shadows had wrapped around him like a net.

Tickled with his own cleverness, the imp skipped around us. "You just fell into my trap!"

Grandpop didn't seem the least bit impressed. "Do you think these shadows can really hold me?"

"Long enough for what I want." The imp kicked the rump of one lion dog and then skipped over to the other one and did the same.

The lion dogs immediately sprang to life, growling with mouths all full of teeth.

"That little boy did it," the imp said, and pointed at me. Snarling, the lion dogs crouched angrily and glared at me.

Grandpop jeered at them. "Shoo. Go away. You're just overgrown doorstops."

The lion dogs growled deep in their throats. It sounded like old gravel rubbing together.

"Please, Grandpop, don't make them madder," I pleaded.

"That's exactly what we need to do," he said. He went on insulting them. "You've got more teeth than sense. And when was the last time you were cleaned? Dust catchers! You're so dirty that pigs wouldn't be seen with you. You should've been ground up for gravel long ago."

He called them whatever else he could come up with. As they listened, their tails whipped back and forth, faster and faster.

Finally, Grandpop called them pigeon benches. That was the last straw. With a lash of their tails, the lion dogs sprang.

Their stone paws thumped heavily against the street as they charged, but they moved as quickly as real animals.

"Hold me up, boy," Grandpop said. His cane clattered through the net onto the street.

Thump, thump, thump went their paws as the lion dogs came nearer and nearer.

The imp's net clung to me, but I managed to get behind Grandpop and wrap my arms around his waist. I wanted to close my eyes, but I couldn't.

Thump, thump, thump. The lion dogs got closer and closer.

"Don't let me drop, boy," Grandpop said.

"I won't," I promised.

When the lion dogs opened their mouths to roar, I smelled wet cement.

Grandpop shot out his right fist. The strands of the net stretched like rubber as his fist went into the

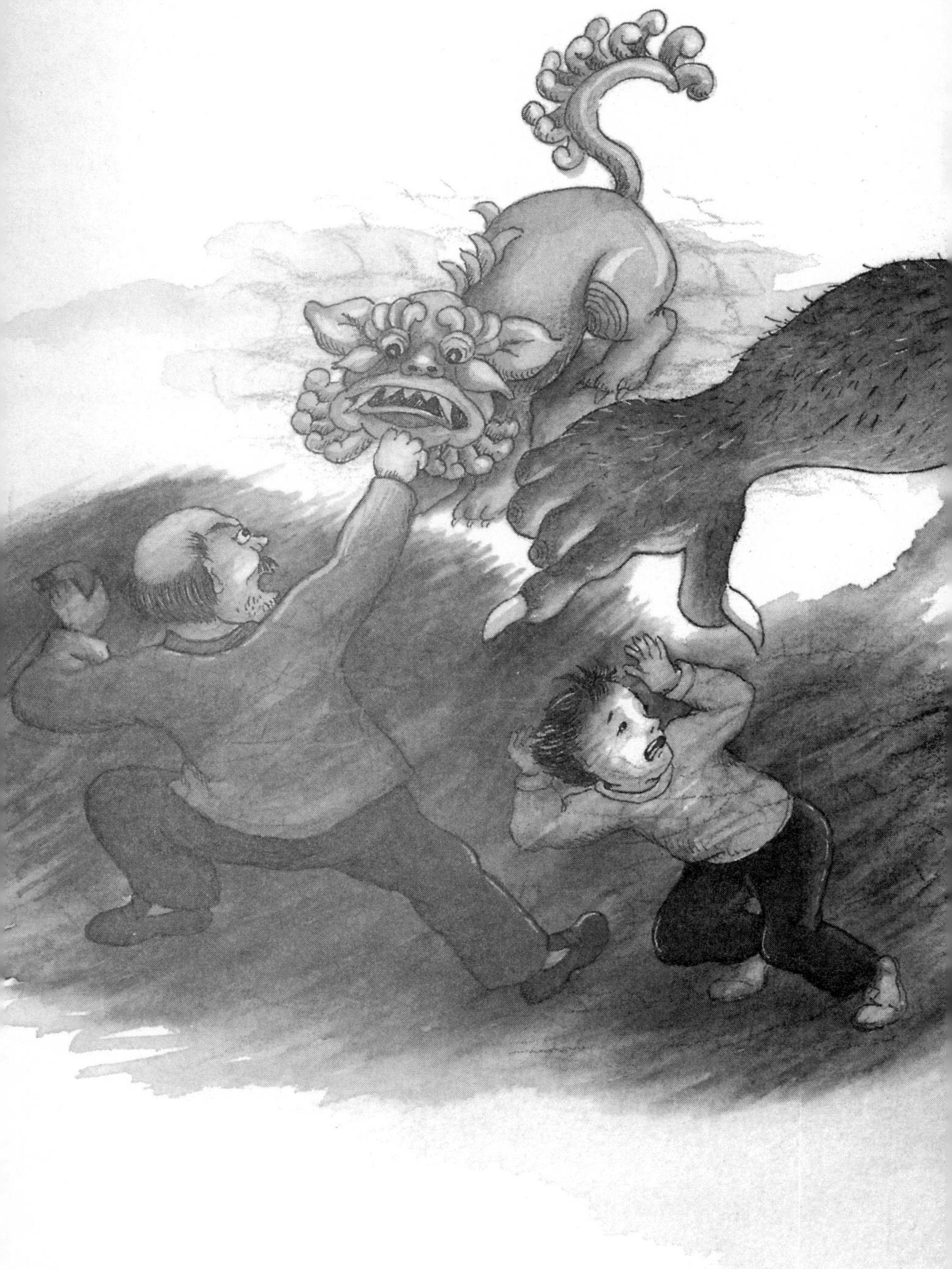

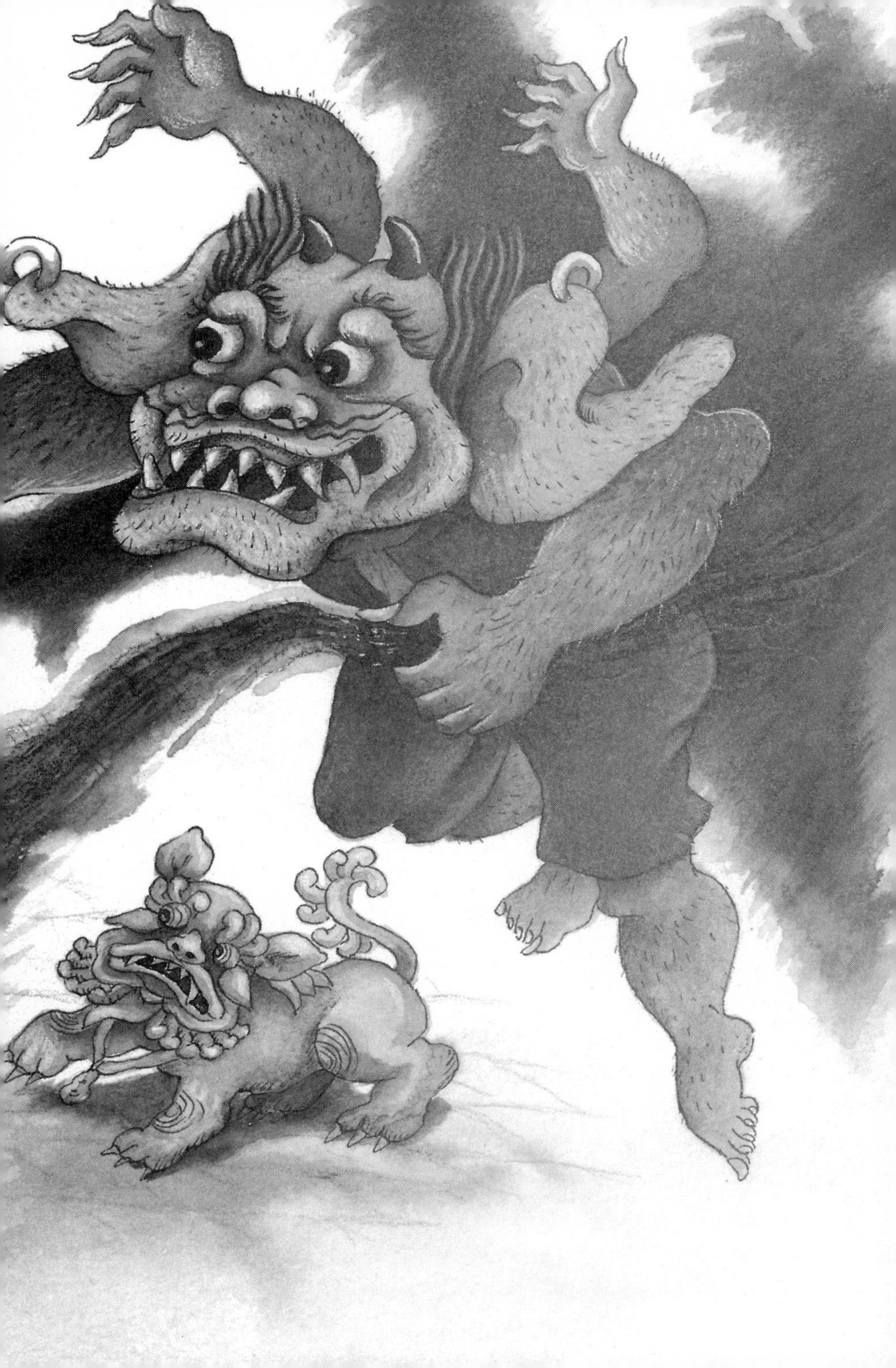

mouth of the first lion dog.

The next moment Grandpop thrust out his left fist into the mouth of the other lion dog.

"Foul, foul!" the imp shouted. "You're not supposed to feed yourself to the lion dogs."

"Keep me standing up, boy," Grandpop ordered. "If I fall, I'll lose my grip, and they'll eat us for sure."

"Why don't they bite you?" I asked.

"I've got hold of their tongues," Grandpop said. But it seemed more like they had him.

"Now hold on, boy," Grandpop said. "This ride's going to get wild."

Puzzled, the lion dogs set their paws down on the street. Growling, they shook their heads and rocked us back and forth.

"I'm going to file a complaint," the outraged imp yelled. "This isn't in the rules."

"That's why I always win," Grandpop said.

As the frightened lion dogs shook their heads frantically, the shadow ropes stretched more and more, and the spaces between them got wider and wider. Soon they looked big enough to step through.

In the meantime, the imp was throwing a tantrum in the street. "Cheater! Swindler!"

Fortunately, the lion dogs wore out before we did. Hanging their heads, they rested. With a tug, Grandpop pulled his hand out of one lion dog's mouth. With a yank, he freed his other hand.

Whimpering, the lion dogs clawed at the shadow ropes that were now caught on their teeth.

Quickly we stepped out of the battered, stretched net. "They're not going to suffocate, are they?" I asked Grandpop.

"No, they can breathe," Grandpop said. "But from now on, they'll be a little more choosy about who they bite."

The disappointed imp had worked himself up into a fury. "If you want something done right, you have to do it yourself," he sputtered. "All in favor?" He raised his four paws. "The ayes have it." The imp slashed the air with knife-sharp claws.

A shadow rope had torn loose from the net in the lion dogs' struggle. Grandpop stood by the tip of the rope. "Pick up my cane and get ready to dodge, boy," he whispered to me.

When I got his cane and gave it to him, Grandpop spoke loudly. "Do you know why imps are easy to catch, boy?"

"No," I said, figuring out Grandpop's plan. He was going to try the same trick he had played on the dogs.

"They never learn," Grandpop said. "They couldn't even find their head with a map."

"I'm going to sue for slander," the imp yelled.

"By the way, do you know what five pounds of ham bones are?" Grandpop asked me loudly.

"No, what?" I said.

"A decorating kit for an imp," Grandpop said. "And do you know what fifty pounds of ham bones are?"

I played my part. "What?" I asked.

"Fifty years of birthday presents for an imp," Grandpop said.

The imp looked hurt. "Liar. My mother only gave them to me one year."

Grandpop went on, "Why did the imp throw the clock out the window? To see time fly!"

As bad as the jokes were, Grandpop knew his audience. In no time, he had the imp frothing at the mouth. Finally, Grandpop asked me, "Do you know why an imp can't pick his nose?"

"Why?" I asked.

"Because he can't make up his mind. He has four index claws and only two nostrils," Grandpop said.

With a howl, the imp charged. I held my breath. Just as the imp reached him, Grandpop shouted, "Now!"

I skipped to the side while Grandpop tripped the imp. The imp's head hit the asphalt hard. While he lay there stunned, Grandpop tied the shadow rope around the imp's ankle.

"Help me roll this imp." Grandpop leaned on his cane. As we pushed the imp along, the shadow rope wrapped itself around him until he was tied up tight in a black cocoon. I couldn't even see the spikes of his hair. The fight was over. Our team had won.

Grandpop stood over the squirming bundle. "It was bad enough to pick a fight with me," he said to the imp inside. "But your real mistake was in attacking my family."

"He sure made a lot of trouble," I said.

Grandpop tucked the bundle under his arm. "I'm used to cleaning up the messes imps make before I catch them. I'll talk to your teachers and Miss Gee and Ah Wong. If they're sensible people, they'll understand," he said.

"What if they're not?" I asked.

Grandpop shrugged. "Then you'll have to put up with them. I've had to put up with a lot of silly people in my time."

That included me. I felt ashamed. "I guess it's hard for people to look at things in more than one way."

"Not everyone can handle it," Grandpop said.

"Maybe you could teach me, though," I said.

"It'll be nice to have a teammate." He stretched out a hand and gripped my shoulder.

"You got one," I promised.

He gave my shoulder a warm squeeze. "I'm counting on you."

Teammates

And with the next breath, my ears popped and I was back in the Square beside the stone table. I could see my face reflected in Grandpop's eyes. "Don't go walking in the clouds, boy. Come back to earth," he said.

Mr. Lee smiled. "You don't want to watch two old men play chess." He was setting out the pieces for a new game.

Nothing seemed to have changed. "How did you do that?" I asked Grandpop. "I thought you couldn't work any magic."

"What magic? Everything's just going back to normal," Grandpop said innocently as he helped Mr. Lee.

I saw Grandpop was sitting on a brand-new silk cushion with green tassels. Sometimes he squirmed as he shifted his weight, and sometimes the cushion squirmed all on its own. It all depended on how you looked at it.

When they were finished, Mr. Lee rubbed his hands. "This time you've met your match, chess wizard. Get ready to lose."

Grandpop folded his arms. "Play, don't brag." As Mr. Lee thought about his first move, Grandpop began to whistle.

I stared at him. "I didn't know you could whistle."

"There's a lot you don't know about your old grandpop," he teased.

I grinned. "But the fun's just beginning for us. Right, teammate?"

"Right," he said as Mr. Lee nudged a piece forward.

With a wink at me, Grandpop made his move.

Author's Note

There are many types of demons in Chinese folklore. The imp in this book represents one of the smaller, mischievous demons. An early story about Chung Kuei as a demon chaser places him in the T'ang dynasty. One afternoon the emperor Ming Huang (A.D. 713–742) found himself harassed by a small, playful demon who introduced himself as "Stealing for the fun of it." The demon's main purpose was to "transform people's joys into sorrows." All of a sudden, Chung Kuei appeared. He stopped the demon from harassing the emperor. Then he told his story to Ming Huang as it has been recounted in this book. Chung Kuei went on to have a long and varied career battling demons of all sizes, a theme that is popular in Chinese painting and literature.